The Gods and their Machines

'Completely fantastical yet totally relevant'

Eoin Colfer,
author of the *Artemis Fowl* trilogy and *The Wish List*

*'A pacy, action-filled plot with very real characters
facing gripping dilemmas'*

Mark O'Sullivan,
Reading Association of Ireland award-winner

D1465028

Born in Dublin, **Oisín McGann** spent his childhood there and in Drogheda, County Louth. He studied at Dún Laoghaire School of Art and Design, and then worked in advertising, design and film animation. He now lives in Drogheda and works as a freelance illustrator and artist. He is the author of two books for younger readers, *Mad Grandad's Flying Saucer* and *Mad Grandad's Robot Garden*. Oisín's latest novel is *The Harvest Tide Project*, the first book in The Archisan Tales, and he is currently finalising the second book in the series, *Under Fragile Stone*.

THE GODS
AND
THEIR MACHINES

Oisín McGann

THE O'BRIEN PRESS
DUBLIN

First published 2004 by The O'Brien Press Ltd,
20 Victoria Road, Dublin 6, Ireland.
Tel: +353 1 4923333; Fax: +353 1 4922777
E-mail: books@obrien.ie
Website: www.obrien.ie
Reprinted 2004.

ISBN: 0-86278-833-1

British Library Cataloguing-in-Publication Data.
A catalogue record for this title is available from the British Library.

The O'Brien Press receives assistance from

2 3 4 5 6
04 05 06 07 08

Editing, typesetting, layout and design: The O'Brien Press Ltd
Printing: Nørhaven Paperback A/S

Acknowledgements

I'd like to thank every writer whose work I've ever read, or seen on screen. Their stories, thoughts and experiences have enriched my life, and there can hardly be a line in this book that was not written under the influence of some other, infinitely better writer.

I owe a debt of gratitude to Mum, Marek, Erika and Darius, and all my friends and family who contributed to shaping and refining *The Gods and Their Machines*, their support has made a big difference in helping me get it right. I also want to thank everyone at O'Brien Press for their enthusiasm, and for their confidence in me. It would be difficult to overstate the importance to a writer of getting their first novel published, and OBP have made it all the more rewarding with their unrelenting passion for books.

I particularly want to thank my editor, Susan, for her deft and diplomatic approach to honing the story; OBP's excellent designer, Emma, for spotting *Mad Grandad*'s potential and for putting up with my ongoing fanaticism; and finally my sister, Kunak, for enforcing the rule of reason whenever any problems came up.

Thanks to all of you.

Oisín.

For my parents, Eileen and Brendan; for their love,
their wisdom, and for understanding
why I never went out and got a proper job.

Twenty

This was not his nightmare. As he found himself behind the controls of an unfamiliar aeroplane, Chamus Aranson instinctively recognised where he was. This was the nightmare that plagued his grandfather's sleep; every detail was exactly as Grandad had described it. He was reliving the plane crash that had crippled the old man fourteen years ago.

It was a routine flight; he was testing a new design, a sleek new monoplane. His route had taken him over the border of Majarak, in the Fringelands. No sooner had Chamus become aware of where he was than he felt the snapping of bullets passing through the fuselage. Somebody was shooting at him from the ground, two hundred feet below. The engine suddenly spat oil and smoke from its vents, and he heard a harsh knocking in the cylinder that told him a piston had been damaged. The engine coughed and stalled. And then the stick went loose and Chamus discovered he had no elevator control. One of the cables must have been cut by a bullet. The powerless aeroplane, weighed down by the heavy engine in its nose, dipped slowly forward and slipped down through the air, plummeting towards the ground, wind tearing at the edges of its wings.

He woke with a gasp, the image of the ground tilting up towards him still filling his vision. His hands were trembling as he sat up and waited for the disorientation to fade. He remembered how his grandfather often said that it was not the memory of the crash itself that haunted him. It was discovering after the crash landing that his legs were trapped by the buckled firewall that separated the cockpit from the engine compartment. It was the sight of orange flames erupting from the engine cowling and the heat and the smell of burning oil. It was the knowledge that his plane, like all modern aircraft, was made of resin-impregnated wood. It was the certainty that he was going to burn to death.

But Thomex Aranson had not died that day. He had been pulled from the crumpled body of the plane by two Majarak farmers, who had seen the aircraft go down. His legs were crushed and he suffered some burns to his hands and arms, but he survived. He never found out who shot at him or why, but it was probably some Fringelander with a chip on his shoulder who liked taking pot-shots at Altima flyers.

Chamus looked at the alarm clock on the chest of drawers beside his bed.

'Bugger!'

He was late; he must have knocked the alarm off in his sleep again. He rolled out of bed, threw off his pyjamas and pulled on his school uniform, jamming his feet into his shoes as he shrugged his blazer on. On his way out of his room, he saw his grandfather's bedroom door was slightly ajar and he peered in. Thomex was rolling from side to side, the old man's face twisted in fear, and Chamus wondered if his grandfather was living through the same nightmare that he had just escaped. He watched for a minute longer, wishing he could do something to ease his grandad's fears. A hand softly clasped his shoulder and his father reached from behind him and closed the door.

'You're going to be late for school,' Kellen said. 'Where are your things? I'll give you a lift to the station.'

'Shouldn't we wake him up?' Chamus asked.

'He barely sleeps as it is. Besides, do you want to be the first person he sees when he wakes up?'

Chamus shook his head. Grandad in a bad mood was not a pretty sight. He grabbed his cap and coat and swung his bag over his shoulder. His mother shoved a bacon sandwich into his hand as he ran for the front door. She never let him leave the house without some kind of breakfast. He took a great big bite out of it once he was settled in the passenger seat of his dad's car. His father grinned at him.

'What have you got today? Flying?'

'Commander Ellese is going to take us up,' Chamus said around the mouthful of sandwich, referring to one of the school's founders, a revered war hero. 'That's if the weather's okay. Otherwise we've got history.'

Kellen glanced up at the sky above the roof of their large, red-brick house; it was a clear blue with wisps of cloud. Perfect flying weather. He started the engine and pulled out onto the road. Kellen had left the air force to take over his father's small business, designing and building planes, and knew his son was itching to get airborne. The Benaldon Preparatory Flying School in Victovia combined pilot training with normal lessons and its students were considered among the elite, destined for the key flying positions in Altima. Kellen hoped that Chamus too would get into the family business, but he knew the boy had his heart set on flying fighters – like every other boy at the school.

They missed the train and the next one was not for twenty minutes. Chamus looked up at the station clock and swore loudly. If he were late he would miss the briefing, and if he missed the briefing he would not be allowed fly.

'Less of that language from you, your mother would have a fit,' his father said, but he could see the disappointment on his son's face. 'Come on, hop in. I don't have to be in until the meeting at ten. I'll drive you.'

Chamus kept looking at his watch as the car sped along the road that ran around the outskirts of the city. It was going to be close.

'Can't we go any faster?' he asked, impatiently.

'This beast can do nearly ninety miles an hour on the straight,' Kellen told him proudly. 'These new two-strokes can really hare along …'

'I meant, can't you *drive* any faster?'

'Yes, Cham. But not fast enough to escape the police. Let's keep it under the speed limit, shall we? We'll get you there on time.'

Chamus idly wondered how a man could have the nerve to be a test pilot and still be afraid of breaking the speed limit. He glanced at his watch again, but it was no comfort.

It was a little after eight when they reached the airfield; the briefing would have already started. Chamus thanked his dad, grabbed his satchel and rushed towards the hangar. He had missed roll call, so he would have to go straight to the briefing room, face the music and hopefully still get his place on the flight plan.

'Aranson!' a voice roared behind him. 'Where d'you think you're going?'

He stopped short and stood ramrod straight, spinning on his heel to face Mr Morthrom, the geography and navigation teacher – a squinty-eyed whippet of a man.

'Sir! I was making my way to the hangar to join my class, sir!'

'If you miss roll call, you don't fly. You know the rules, Aranson.'

Chamus nodded. He had been hoping to bypass that particular rule. But there was no chance with Morthrom.

'Commander Ellese has your class this morning, but it seems you are to miss the honour of flying with him. Go and inform him that you are here and that you will await your class's return in the library. I shall give you some exercises to do.'

'Yes, sir!' Chamus could hardly keep the disappointment from his face. They had not flown for two weeks because of bad weather during their flying periods. Ellese was notorious for breaking the rules, which made him popular with the students. Maybe he would still let him go up with the class. But Cham did not fancy his chances once Morthrom had made up his mind.

As he trudged the last hundred yards to the training planes hangar, a man hurried past him. He glanced back as he passed, and several expressions seemed to ripple across his face at once, so quickly that Chamus thought he had imagined it. There was a sound like whispering and Chamus stopped for a moment and looked around, puzzled, but could not see anyone else about. Access to the hangar was restricted and he didn't recognise the man, but he looked like a Fringelander. The only ones who worked in the school were caretakers. Cham wondered if this man was new. The stranger was walking very fast and disappeared from sight into the darkness of the big corrugated sheet metal and concrete building. Chamus followed him in and traced his fingertips along the leading edge of the wing of a trainer before making his way to the briefing room.

There were raised voices coming from beyond the doorway. He could hear Ellese demanding to know who the stranger was and what he was doing there. Another voice, one that must be that of the Fringelander, was shouting in a strange language, almost chanting. Chamus walked up to the doorway and peered inside. The stranger was standing in front of Ellese's desk, with the instructor facing him behind it. The boys of Cham's class were sitting at their desks watching the spectacle. The two men were glaring at each other, then the stranger became abruptly silent, his head tilted upwards, his mouth wide open, his eyes rolled back. Even as this was happening, the Fringelander blurred and disappeared, and as he did, the walls of the briefing room faded away, the noticeboards and regulation blue walls turning transparent and vanishing from view.

Chamus went suddenly numb. The classroom was disappearing around him. He found himself standing in an open street, surrounded by adobe buildings. Around him, people were hurrying into their houses, but his class still sat at their desks in the middle of the street, staring at the open, grey sky in shock. There was the sound of aeroplanes overhead and he heard the torn whistle of bombs falling. An object plummeted down and struck just where the stranger had been standing before he had vanished. The object was a metal javelin, with a barrel-shaped section at its waist, holes running up its side and fins on its tail. Chamus was bewildered. What was going on? They had been in the hangar. How could they suddenly have ended up in a street he had never seen before? It was as if they were all sharing some vivid, waking dream. Then Chamus realised what the javelin was; his heart leapt into his throat. It was a sireniser.

He must have started running, for suddenly the village faded away and he was in the main part of the hangar again. His classmates were still in the briefing room behind him. He did not think about them. He dodged around the parked training planes, instinctively sprinting for open space. He could only have seconds before the sireniser went off. The door was getting wider, but he felt nothing, heard nothing. He had just made it out the door and looked up to see the big, wide sky, when a wall of sound slammed into him and threw him across the concrete apron. The noise was like nothing he had ever heard, it had no pitch, no quality – it just sounded like the end of the world.

+   +   +   +

Chamus did not know what was going on. His first sensation was a massive headache and then there was a ringing in his ears. As he opened his eyes, he became aware that the ringing was the only thing he could hear. There were men in different kinds of uniform around him, some wearing ear-protectors. He could see them talking to each other, see their mouths moving, but he could not hear a thing over the ringing. Judging by the view, he was lying on his back. He went to move his head, and discovered he too was wearing headgear. He should still have been able to hear something. The headache wanted to stay where it was, so he let it and just lay still.

One of the men, in the uniform of an air force medical officer, noticed he was awake and looked down at him with an expression of concern. He lifted his ear protectors carefully, then took them off and leaned forward to listen.

'Am I deaf?' he asked the man, his voice sounding as if he were speaking into the back of his skull.

The man shook his head. He wrote out something on a piece of paper and then showed it to Chamus. His vision was blurred and it hurt to focus on anything, but he could just make it out.

'Your eardrums are intact and your hearing will come back in time,' it read. 'You're going to be alright.'

He nodded slightly to show he understood, but he could only remember flashes of what had happened. He let his head roll gently to the side and looked at the hangar. It was still standing, but only just. The metal girders of the roof had buckled and collapsed; the concrete walls were teetering under the weight of the rest of the structure. Through the huge doorway, he could see that the shockwaves from the sound weapon had wrought devastation on the aircraft and equipment inside – all the work of a weapon that had seemed to appear out of nowhere, as part of some bizarre vision cast by an unknown Fringelander. He could only remember snatches of what had happened and none of it made sense.

'The others?' he asked.

The medical officer shook his head. Chamus closed his eyes and wished the world away from him. He felt a needle prick his arm and then felt nothing more.

 # Πineteeп

Riadni Mocranen's older brother stopped laughing the instant her shinbone connected sharply with his testicles. Suddenly the sight of seeing her fall flat on her back while trying to mount her horse wasn't so funny. He folded up and crumpled to the ground with tears in his eyes. Riadni patted the dust off the back of her tunic and trousers, straightened her headscarf and wig and walked back to Rumbler, the old piebald stallion, who waited patiently for her to finish her business. Barra, her brother, had loosened the girth, the strap holding the saddle to the horse's body, so when she put her foot in the stirrup and swung her other leg up over the horse's back, the saddle slid sideways, causing the stirrup to slip round under the horse's belly. She had hit the ground like a sack of potatoes.

Barra would be on the ground for a while longer, though. She tightened the girth and leapt up on Rumbler's back. The other boys, including her younger brother, Jarin, kept a respectful distance as she rode by. She knew her face-paint would be smeared and her wig dusty, but she kept her chin up and her back straight and looked at them with disdain as she trotted past them, then gritted her teeth and tapped her heels against her horse's sides for a gallop home.

Rumbler was old, easily the oldest horse in Kemsemet. He had been her father's favourite mount, but when his age had started to show, her father had given him up for a younger dapple-grey. Sostas Mocranen had planned to make some money out of the old warhorse, using him to cover mares while his seed was still good, and then putting him down. But Riadni had begged him relentlessly to give her the old horse. Sostas would have found the idea of any other girl owning a horse ridiculous, but Riadni did not seem to be growing out of her tomboy ways and she had learned to ride right along with her brothers. And if he could not make her a good daughter, he could at least give her the chance to be a good son. So he had borne the laughter of his neighbours, and had given Riadni his old horse. She and Rumbler had taken to each other immediately, and Rumbler, now that he did not have to carry the weight of her father, showed he still had plenty of life in him.

Above the beat of the horse's hooves, she heard a droning noise and lifted her head to see a group of aeroplanes flying high overhead. Altimans. She and her brothers had come out to the far side of town to where Brother Fazekiel, the local priest was leading a protest against an Altiman-owned factory that was pumping noxious clouds of gas out over the area. It had been fun to join in the shouting. She had never met an Altiman, but her father and his friends talked about them all the time. She often saw their aircraft, however, sometimes in groups like these, sometimes alone. They lived in the region of plateaux to the north-west and her father said they did not like to travel down into Bartokhrin; they flew over it because they thought it dirty and primitive. From up there, the people of Altima could look down on their neighbours without having to consort with them. She slowed Rumbler to a walk, so that she could watch the aircraft. She thought that there was something godlike about them, the way they had conquered the skies, the way they did not need to walk on the ground anymore. There were eight of them, each with two engines, mounted on the wings. The lead plane turned into a dive and the others followed, flowing as one, like a flock of birds. They were closer now, nearly over the village of Yered on the other side of the hill and she could see details, their black tops and silver undersides, the sharp things on the front where the propellers would be if they weren't going too fast to see, the glass windows where the pilots looked out, the hatches open in their bellies …

She pulled gently on the reins, bringing Rumbler to a halt. There were things falling out of the planes. Her breath caught in her throat. Yered was being bombed. It was less than a dozen miles from home. She had never seen a bombing before; somehow it did not look as dramatic as she had thought it would from all the stories she had heard. There was a mountain ridge between her and the village, but even so, she was surprised that there was no smoke or fire visible. She felt sorry for the people in Yered, but excited too. It was too far away to affect her family, but what a story to tell over dinner!

She considered riding out there to see the damage and perhaps even help if she could. But one look at the sun told her she was already late and Rumbler was tired. Her wig was hot and heavy on her head and she pulled it off to let the faint breeze run its cool breath through her dark hair. It was forbidden for her to remove her wig in public, or even to leave home without her face made up, but she had little time for tradition and 'forgot' whenever she could get away with it. She flicked the reins and Rumbler started walking again towards town. She wanted to get home before Barra and Jarin. Just so they didn't blab the story to anyone at home about her falling off the horse before she could tell it her way.

It was summer and the road was dusty, the green grass in the fields either side beginning to burn to an arid yellow. The air was dry and the rocky hills hazy in the evening heat. Riadni pulled a water canteen from her saddle and gulped some down. It was warm but still refreshing. She poured some into her cupped hand and sprinkled it on the back of Rumbler's neck. There was a rattle of hooves on the road behind her and she turned, expecting to see her brothers giving chase. But it wasn't her brothers; there were men racing towards her on powerful warhorses. With a start, she realised that she was not wearing her wig. She quickly pulled it on and straightened it as best she could, flicking the braids over her shoulders and patting the curls back into place.

The horses were being ridden hard. Their coats were lathered and froth dripped from their mouths, their hooves drumming the dust into a cloud that trailed behind them. There were eight men, all armed with rifles or muskets, swords and knives, all riding with a sense of urgency. In the middle of the group was a man she recognised, a friend of her father's, Lakrem Elbeth. The others rode in a circle around him so as to shelter him. Riadni steered Rumbler off the road to get out of their way and they rushed past, losing her in their dust cloud. She tasted grit, swilled some spit around her mouth and let it fly. It was a beauty. Her mother would have slapped her good and hard for that one. She let the dust settle and continued on her way. She was hungry now and eager to get home.

+ + + +

The eight horses were waiting for her, tied to the rail outside the two-storey, plastered adobe house. They were still panting and their heads hung with exhaustion. Kyumeth Mocranen was straining tea through a cloth when Riadni trotted into the yard. She saw her daughter through the kitchen window and waved her inside. There was a man she didn't know sitting in the corner of the kitchen. He looked up when Riadni came in and took off her boots, then went back to reading the Kes, one of the three books of Shanna.

'Were you riding the horse or carrying it?' her mother snorted. 'You look a mess. Clean yourself up quickly and help me serve supper. We have guests.'

Riadni filled a basin from the pitcher on the table and took it upstairs to her room. She stripped off her riding clothes and washed using the basin, then sprinkled some perfumed water from a jar onto her bare feet. There weren't many dresses in her cupboard, and the ones she had were worn and uncared for. She slipped into a long, light, loosely fitting, raw-cotton dress that covered her from neck to ankles and sat cross-legged in front of the mirror on the floor to paint her face with the stylised make-up, a white face with sharp, curving eyebrows, heavy eyeliner, high, rouged cheekbones and deep red lips. Apart from her father and her brothers, the next man to see her without this religious mask would be her husband (whoever that would be) on their wedding night. The Bartokhrians worshipped the she-god, Shanna, and Shanneyan women had always to be dressed, coiffed and painted in the image of Shanna, for her image would protect their virtue. Riadni had started wearing the wigs and make-up when she turned fourteen, almost a year ago, and she still hated them. Taking her dress wig from its stand, she arranged it carefully on her head and stared at herself in the mirror. Some day she would rid herself of this nonsense.

Lakrem Elbeth was with her father in the large gathering room at the back of the house. Sitting protectively around him were six more men with lean bodies and hard eyes. She noticed with disgust that they had not taken off their riding cloaks or boots. Even their wide-brimmed hats still hung down their backs. She was the one who would have to clean that floor this evening, after they had left and taken their bad manners with them.

'Ah, young Riadni!' Elbeth turned to her as she walked in with a tray of tea and honey pastries. 'How enchanting you look in a dress! And here I thought it was a boy wearing a hairpiece that we passed on the road.'

There were some loyal chuckles from the other men and her father smiled uncomfortably. Riadni bowed, but remained silent. She laid the tray on the low table in front of Elbeth and left the room. But once out of sight, she hung back by the doorway to listen to what was being said. Her mother saw her, but said nothing. Riadni was old enough now to start learning about the world of men – provided she was discreet about it.

'So, you see, old friend,' Elbeth was saying, 'with the attack on Yered, the Altimans have shown us that they have no mercy for those who speak out against them. Our old camp has become too dangerous; we need a safe place to stay, to plan and to train our new recruits.'

'I understand, Lakrem,' she heard her father say, 'but you said it yourself. They laid waste to Yered. You say they used the flail bombs, the ones that scar all those who survive, so that they are marked for life. In Jermanya, it was the killing sound; they had to desert the village and the wounded until it died away. These weapons they use against us don't know the difference between men, women and children. And Brother Fazekiel tells me that every village that harbours rebels is targeted. If it was just my own life you were asking me to risk, you know I wouldn't hesitate. But my family …'

'I know, I know, Sostas,' Elbeth said soothingly, 'but it will only be for a while, until we find a more permanent base. Fazekiel is an alarmist, he means well, but he is weak-willed. He thinks that protest marches and negotiations can win the peace, as if the politicians would have anything to negotiate with, without our operations against the cities. We need somewhere with cover, where their aeroplanes can't see us – somewhere we can keep horses and store weapons and supplies. It won't be for long, I promise you. And you won't even know we're there.'

Riadni glanced up at her mother and thought about what she was hearing. So those planes that had bombed Yered had been after Elbeth! The thought frightened and thrilled her. They had been after Elbeth and his men and now he wanted to set up camp on her father's land. She knew that Elbeth had saved her father's life once, long ago. The older man talked as if he did not expect any more argument from his host, and yet Riadni's father was not a man to be pushed around. Lakrem was an important member of the Hadram Cassal, a group of rebels that fought against the Altimans' control of Bartokhrin. Having them here would be exciting. Riadni might get to learn some riding techniques, or even how to shoot or use a sword. Many of the men in Hadram Cassal had travelled to other lands, some even to the cities in Altima and she ached to hear the stories of life there. But she was sure that her father would not allow Elbeth to do anything that would put his family in danger.

'Alright,' Sostas Mocranen sighed, 'you can set up camp in the caves in Sleeping Hill. But only for a few weeks. Every day you stay here is a risk to us all.'

'You have my word, Sostas,' Elbeth's voice smiled. 'We'll be gone before you know it.'

+ + + +

It was quiet in the exam hall and Chamus could not concentrate. It had taken a few weeks for the ringing in his ears to disappear completely, but even then he was certain he could still hear something when everything was quiet around him. That had been four months ago. Now, in the summer navigation exam, over the mouse-like scratch of fountain pens and grease pencils, and the leafy rasp of pages being turned, a murmuring tickled at the very edge of his hearing. It was as if someone at the back of the hall was whispering something intended for him, but was saying it too quietly for him to hear it. Trying to ignore the sound, he turned his attention back to the exam paper:

'Q.23 – Give the difference, in feet, between the standard nautical mile and the statute mile,' it read, 'and state the formulae for converting one to the other.'

Morthrom wandered into his field of vision, reading a newspaper. On the front page was a report on the latest terrorist attack. Chamus found himself trying to see the photograph that accompanied the article and looked down quickly before Morthrom could catch him not paying attention to the test. He was normally good with numbers, but he couldn't remember the lengths of either type of mile. He skipped the question, deciding to go back to it later:

'Q.24 – Define an isogonal and explain its relevance in instrument flying.'

Isothermal was temperature, what was isogonal? Magnetic? He rubbed his eyes. Maybe he should go back to that one too. The sound continued whispering in the back of his head. He had not mentioned it to the doctor who had been examining him since the attack on the hangar. He did not want people to think he was hearing voices. It was bad enough trying to fit into a new class, being the boy no one wanted to talk to. What did you say to someone who had survived an attack that had killed all his friends?

Against the doctor's advice, he had left the hospital and gone back to the hangar to see the clean-up crews dig out the broken bodies. He blocked the thought of what he had seen there from his mind:

'Q.25 – Calculate the velocity of an aircraft travelling south at an airspeed of sixty knots against an easterly wind of fifteen knots.'

It had not been the only attack that day. Five different men had walked into five different places: the city hall, a main shopping street, the stock exchange, the central court … crowded, public places, and had dealt out death by means that still baffled the authorities. The results resembled weapons created in Altima. Two sirenisers, a poison-gas canister, a flail bomb and an acid grenade. Thirty-two people had died altogether (not including the five suicidal maniacs) and dozens had been injured. But according to witnesses, none of the men had carried any weapons, and every witness had seen nightmarish visions at the moment of detonation. And each had been in the same kind of trance-like state that Chamus had seen for himself. All of the terrorists had died with their victims. People were whispering a new word from the Fringelands: *mortiphas* – the power to summon death from the past.

There had been assassinations before, but nothing like this. A group called the Hadram Cassal had claimed responsibility, saying they were acting to end Altima's domination of the Fringelands, that they were the avenging hands of martyrs from centuries past. As if Altima had not been pulling the Fringelands out of one famine, drought, or war after another for years. He gritted his teeth even now to think of their stupidity. He desperately wanted to hurt somebody for what had happened, to make somebody pay. Violent fantasies played themselves out in his mind, both shocking and satisfying him.

'Mr Aranson,' a sharp voice broke into his thoughts, 'are we keeping you from something?'

Chamus came to his senses with a start. He was back in the navigation exam. Glancing at the clock he saw that he had only half an hour left, and he had skipped most of the questions. He bowed his head over the exam paper and tried to block out the whispering that babbled persistently just beyond the reach of his ears.

+ + + +

Chamus handed over his half-answered exam sheet when Morthrom clapped his hands to call time, then he picked up his satchel and walked out. Down one end of the corridor, he saw a group of boys crowding around Vel Sillian. Sillian, a tall, dark-haired, athletic-looking lad, had used the commotion at the end of the exam to swipe Morthrom's newspaper and now everyone wanted a look.

'The bastards hit the National Library on Whalpot Road,' Sillian was saying. 'What kind of sick pigs firebomb a *library*? I'm two years away from the academy, and then my dad's going to see I get into a front-line unit. I'm going to give them hell when I get out there.'

He saw Chamus coming up the hall.

'Hey, Cham, bet you're dying to get out there and lay down some fire! After what they did to your mates, you're probably ready to strafe the lot of 'em.'

Chamus found all the boys looking expectantly at him, as if waiting for a suitably vengeful reply. He knew he should reel out some jock talk, rant about machine-gunning or rocketing a rebel camp, or something. And he wanted to show how he felt, but listening to these boys, it just came out sounding like lines from a comic story. He nodded to Sillian and held out his hand for the paper. The taller boy gave it to him and Chamus read the article.

'The scum are all around us, living here, working here. It could be any one of us next,' Sillian said as he watched Chamus read. 'We should just get rid of the lot of 'em, turf 'em out. Let them rot in their own soddin' country.'

'Then who would we get to clean our toilets?' Chamus muttered, and the other boys laughed. He kept reading.

The town of Yered, in Bartokhrin, had been marked as harbouring terrorists and the air force had laid a blanket of flail bombs over it in retaliation for the attack on the library. There were other articles, one discussing the possibility of war, one giving a one-hundred-and-fifty-word summary of the Fringelands' religion and another about some disease that had broken out in Bartokhrin.

There had been a score of suicide attacks since the first wave, and they were all starting to read alike. The assassins had become known as 'the Haunted', because it was said that they carried death with them. They were rumoured to have superhuman strength and endurance, and supernatural senses. But even with reports of such menacing powers, most people still considered them as merely madmen and fanatics. Chamus was surprised at how normal it had all become. As if walking into a library and unleashing the force of an acid grenade was the kind of thing that was expected from Fringelanders. People had stopped being shocked at what men could do to themselves, and to other people, because it happened all the time. Fringelanders had their terrorists and it was Altima's duty to wipe them out. Wipe them out like rats. How else could you deal with madmen who killed for no reason? He found himself gritting his teeth again and realised he was crumpling the paper in his clenched fists. Looking up at the other boys, he saw something in their eyes as they stared at him – not the frustration he felt, or sympathy for the people who had lost someone that day. They were gazing at him as if his tightly bunched fists were his initiation into some kind of gang. He handed back the paper and walked around to the corridor that led to the assembly yard.

As he walked down past the bank of metal lockers, he saw that one was standing open. It was his locker. He hurried up to it and looked inside. Somebody had rifled through his things. He searched through them and was surprised to find that nothing was missing. The most valuable items, such as his navigation instruments and log-book, were still there, along with the swing records he had borrowed from Roddins. The flimsy metal door had been prised open, probably with a crowbar or something similar, and yet the thief had not taken a thing. And then he realised that there was something missing – one of the photographs that had been stuck to the inside of the door. He frowned. Why would anyone steal a photo and leave all the valuable stuff? Maybe it had just fallen off the door as they searched the locker and then got swept up or kicked away. He turned and checked the floor around him, but there was no sign of it. Chamus shook his head and cleared out the locker, squeezing most of his things into his already bulging schoolbag and tucking the records under his arm.

The caretaker's office was near the entrance to the building, so he was passing it on his way out. He would tell Shamiel about the locker if he saw him. Not that he wanted to; the gnarled old grouch from Bartokhrin took every bit of vandalism in the school personally and even the other Fringelanders who worked under him feared him. His roars could regularly be heard up and down the corridors of the school buildings. But it was better to get it over with now, then face questions later. The service window was closed when he reached the main hall. Shamiel was probably off working in some other part of the school, but Chamus decided to knock anyway. There was no answer, so he tried the door. It opened and he peered in. The head caretaker was sitting at his desk, its surface cluttered with an assortment of keys, fixtures, electrical bits and pieces, and papers stained with tea rings. He had one hand up to his face and was so intent on a piece of paper in the other hand, that he had not even noticed Chamus look in. With a tentative tap, Chamus got his attention and he was taken aback to see tears on the cantankerous Fringelander's face.

'What do you want, boy?' Shamiel asked, his voice rasping, but lacking its normal growl.

'Someone's broken into my locker, Mr Shamiel. They've damaged the door and the lock.'

He braced himself for the tirade: how it was probably his fault and didn't Shamiel have enough to do around here without boys not looking after their lockers and why did nobody have respect for this school anymore … but it didn't come. The caretaker just nodded and turned back to the letter in his hand.

'I'll sort it tomorrow,' he said quietly.

'Mr Shamiel? Are you alright?'

Chamus could see the paper from where he was standing; it was a telegram. He couldn't read most of it, but he recognised the word 'Yered'. He had seen it somewhere before, but could not place where. Then he remembered, the town in the Fringelands that had been bombed. Had Shamiel known someone there?

'I'll sort it tomorrow,' the old caretaker repeated and gave him a baleful look.

Chamus nodded and closed the door.

'What are you hanging about for, Aranson?' a familiar voice asked from behind him.

He turned around, standing wearily to attention.

'Someone broke into my locker, Mr Morthrom. I was reporting it to Mr Shamiel, sir.'

'I see.'

'Mr Shamiel looks upset, sir,' Chamus added softly. 'Is he alright?'

Part of him was sympathetic, but the vindictive side of him wanted to hear if the old goat had received some bad news.

'How should I know?' the teacher replied. 'Mr Shamiel's problems are his own business.'

He took Chamus's arm and led him away from the door.

'You'd do well not to concern yourself with the likes of him,' Morthrom muttered. 'The only reason the whole lot of 'em haven't been fired since these attacks started is because he's been here longer than the bloody building has. Steer clear of them.'

'But he has nothing to do with the terrorists, does he, sir? I mean, the police held him for a week after the hangar was hit and they didn't find anything on him. And he only got out because the headmaster insisted–'

'They're not stupid, you know, boy. You can see that, you know what I mean, you've suffered at their hands. They've got an animal cunning. They cover their tracks well. Some of the other teachers and I have already begun taking measures to see he and the others are removed. They're watching us, while they clean our windows and mop our floors. You've got to keep your eyes open, boy, because one day they're going to try and overturn this great country, and we must be prepared.' He looked around as they walked outside. 'We've made it too easy for them. Given them the same rights as a normal person, let them get educated in our schools. We'll be letting them *vote* soon, for God's sake. You wait and see!'

He turned and put his hands on Chamus's shoulders.

'I know what you're thinking, boy. You're thinking, "this old sod's lost it". But what I'm telling you is the hard truth. I'm not a bigot, I'm a reasonable man, but I'm not afraid to speak the truth, unpopular though it may be. Look at the way they put some kind of curse on their assassins, some ungodly power from the dead! Black magic, devil worship, that's what they believe in, that's what's important to them. And they're jealous of what we have, but they're still just too damned primitive to achieve it themselves, so they don't see why we should have it either. That's what it comes down to, boy. We're victims, victims of envy.'

Chamus pulled the strap of his satchel onto his shoulder, so Morthrom had to move his hand.

'I have to go, sir, I'll miss the train.'

'You go on, boy. But remember what I said. We have to be prepared. Keep your eyes open.'

'Yes, sir. Thank you, sir.'

Morthrom nodded and turned to walk back inside. Chamus waited until he had gone inside before heading for the gate. He didn't like the man. He was obviously a bit paranoid, but some of what he said made sense. The terror of the attack in the hangar played on his mind and he thought about the Fringelanders who worked at the school, and who worked in so many of the down-and-dirty jobs around the city. They were everywhere. A four-engine bomber passed overhead, its glass bubble of a cockpit and bulging gunner's turret like the eye of an insect, its shadow flitting along the ground of the yard like a wraith. He watched it disappear over the roof of a tram depot and stared at the empty sky for a while. In the quiet hole left behind its engines, he heard the murmuring again. He strode out of the yard and made for the comforting noise of the railway station.

# Eighteen

Thomex Aranson sat in his wheelchair, listening to organ music on his record player. He was in the converted dining room at the back of the house, working on his model railway, which took up most of the large room and a sizeable chunk of the house's electricity bill. Chamus loved that train set and the landscapes that his grandfather created to run the trains through. All the bridges, grassy hills, and brick and stone buildings were made from scratch, using papier mâché, wood and other bits and pieces. Model animals, cotton-wool bushes and pipe-cleaner trees added a touch of nature to the environment. And, of course, there was an aerodrome, complete with model aeroplanes. His grandfather put the trains together himself, making bodies to fit over the working parts. The planes were perfectly scaled, hand-built models, made to help in the design of aircraft that his workshops would build.

Chamus walked through into the 'railway room' and sat down by the side of the massive table. He was sitting near the area that mimicked the Fringelands' landscape, set lower than the main area, which was raised to imitate the group of plateaux that made up the state of Altima. The Fringelands' section was open and wild, with few roads and a single railway line winding up into rocky, papier mâché hills. He watched a miniature of one of the new diesel locomotives chatter along the line, waiting for his grandfather to finish gluing the roof to a passenger car.

'How was school?' Thomex asked, turning down the music.

Chamus shrugged. It was the kind of question adults always asked. As if every day in school wasn't the same as every other day – unless there was flying. No two flying days were ever alike.

'We didn't fly,' he said simply. 'Navigation exam.'

'How did you do?'

'Not very well. I couldn't remember how long a nautical mile was. Or name half the stars. I think I failed.'

His grandfather snorted.

'Used to learn all that stuff in the cockpit. You learned it faster when mistakes got you lost. Remember once, when I was starting out, I got latitude and longitude mixed up, reading coordinates. Was looking for a landing strip and found a pig farm.'

'What happened?' Chamus asked.

'Had to land in the field, was out of fuel. Scared the pigs witless, farmer came out to me with a pitchfork, threatened to skewer me. Calmed him down in the end, walked to a nearby town for some fuel and came back. But he was still mightily annoyed about me scarin' his swine. He made me buy a small pig before he'd let me take off. So, I put the pig in the front seat, strapped it in and took off. They say pigs are clean animals, even though they live in muck, but I can tell you that a terrified pig can produce plenty of muck all by itself. That was a hairy flight that one, with a screaming pig thrashing around and dirtying itself in the front seat. I had to punch a hole in the floor and clean the cockpit out with a hose when I got back. Cockpits don't come equipped with drainpipes. The plane was that old rag-wing I started out with and the smell soaked into the canvas walls. It stunk for weeks. Everyone had a good laugh too, at the sight of my co-pilot there with his snout and his curly tail. They put a pair of flying goggles on him and made him the company mascot for a while. But he got eaten some time later, as I remember. Anyway, I never got latitude and longitude mixed up again.'

Chamus sat listening with a smile on his face. Grandad always had good stories.

'Grandad,' he piped up, 'have you ever been out in the Fringelands? Apart from when you crashed, I mean.'

'You mean on the ground? Years ago,' the old man said. 'It was interesting, an experience, if you want to call it that. Flew missions during the Separation War over Nathelem, of course. Stayed with the air force after the war, flying transports. Had to fly people out to airfields out in Bartokhrin and Majarak. Traders and such like, some tourists too. The Fringelanders are a hostile lot. Don't like us much – at least not the lads in the air force. They put up with people who are bringing in business, but then they resent the same folks for coming in and throwing money around. Get offended easily, and you can't always figure out why.

'The religious ones are the worst and they're pretty much

all religious. Like the terrorists, they think God's on their side. Or at least their god ... or goddess, or whatever it is. They're always having a go at Altima and the way we live, but then thousands of 'em are happy enough to come here looking for work. It's hard to tell 'em apart, the ones who want to kill us all and the ones who just don't like us. They live hard, savage lives and it's made 'em hard and savage themselves.'

Listening to his grandfather, Chamus found himself thinking of the Fringelanders he knew, men and women who had come to the city to work. He had never really thought of them as savage. But then maybe he had been afraid to think badly of them, because his mother and father were always telling him not to judge people because of where they came from, or what they looked like. Maybe he had assumed they were all decent and peaceful, because to think they weren't was to be racist. He remembered what Morthrom had said and wondered where the line was between racism and honesty.

His mother called them from the kitchen, telling them that dinner was ready. Chamus pushed his grandfather's wheelchair down the hall and breathed in the smells of lamb chops, mint sauce and potatoes. He sat down at his father's side at the table and noticed the newspaper in his hands. On the front page was the headline, 'Mystery Plague Sweeps Across Bartokhrin'. With any luck, Chamus mused, it'll wipe the bloody country clean.

+ + + +

The belasto was a set of three weighted balls, each attached to the end of a piece of cord; the other ends of the cords tied together in a three-way knot. When thrown with skill, the balls stretched the spinning cords taut and wrapped them around the neck, or legs, of an animal. Riadni watched the drim deer topple over as her belasto tied up its rear legs. It was an excellent throw; her belasto only had wooden training weights and would not normally have brought down a deer. But she had practised hard with them, annoyed that all her brothers, even Jarin, had moved on to the steel weights of a hunter.

'Good,' her father nodded, urging his horse forward. 'Your throws are getting better, but you should go for the neck on the smaller animals.'

He set off at a trot, holding on with just his knees and feet as he fed powder into his musket. Riadni watched and knew he was showing off for her. He could have loaded his gun while he waited for her to make her throw. Rumbler took off after the other horse without waiting to be told. The deer was struggling to get to its feet, its sharp-pronged horns thrashing dangerously. Sostas aimed his musket and fired at the gallop, hitting the deer square in the head – showing off again. Riadni could not help but give a smile.

She slowed Rumbler down and vaulted lightly from his back. Unwinding the belasto, she looped it back around her waist where it was carried and helped her father hoist the carcass onto the back of his horse. She made to get back on Rumbler's back, but Sostas took hold of the old warhorse's bridle and stroked his neck. She stopped and looked at him.

'These men, the ones who are coming to stay on our land,' he said, 'I want you to stay away from them.'

'Yes, of course, Papa,' she replied, then turned to put her foot in the stirrup.

'Listen to me when I'm talking to you, girl,' his voice had an edge to it. She froze, and swivelled back to face him.

'I know you'll want to go and see what they're doing out there, but you are not to go near them. I don't want you looking for them, I don't want you talking to them, I don't even want you to mention them to anyone. Is that clear?'

'Yes,' Riadni leaned against her horse, looking under the fringe of her wig at her father. 'If you're so unhappy having them here, why are you letting them stay?'

As she said it, she caught the sharp look he gave her and she remembered again how much he let her get away with compared with the other girls' fathers. He gazed out towards Sleeping Hill, where even now the Hadram Cassal were making camp. He had seen Altiman fighters in the sky that morning, and the sight had left him feeling anxious.

'There are things that have to be done sometimes, Riadni, that are not right. Some people, like the priest, Brother Fazekiel, believe that the Altimans can be reasoned with, that they hate us because they don't understand us and all it will take to sort out this mess is for both sides to sit down and talk. But peaceful means will only get you so far. There are times when we have to do horrible things in order to be free to live a decent life. You have to kill to eat. You have to fight to win peace. And Shanna knows, sometimes you have to do much worse things just to be left alone by people who would take away everything that is important to you. Lakrem Elbeth and his men have the courage to do these things. There is a great cost to them. They give their lives for us. I would help them in any way I can. But I do not want you, or the boys, involved. If there is one reason for believing in their fight, it is so that the five of you will have a better future than your mother and I. Because Lakrem Elbeth and his men have no future – other than a place in history. Where they go, our enemies will follow, they bring danger like a dog brings its tail. Now, promise me that you will have nothing to do with them.'

'I promise, Papa.'

+ + + +

Sostas Mocranen split away from his daughter on his way home to visit the caves where Elbeth and his men were settling in. He told Riadni to go straight home, but she decided to make the most of the fresh afternoon and let Rumbler have his head. The old warhorse set off at a gallop and Riadni, careful to look around and check that nobody could see her, pulled off her headscarf and wig so that her long, dark hair could whip free in the wind.

Rumbler's feet pounded away, but his movement was light and easy, eating up the distance to the hills ahead of her. She hunched low and forward, her behind barely touching the saddle as she leaned her weight into the run, her body moving in time with the horse's strides. She would ride along the trail in the foothills and avoid the road, and people, for as long as possible. Rumbler found the narrow trail that cut up into the rock face and followed it, anticipating her thoughts without her having to steer him. There was a sharp turn in the gully and Rumbler suddenly skidded to a halt, nearly throwing her. She was about to shout at him when she heard the sound of a horse coming from the other direction. She shouted to warn them that she was there.

'Hey! Watch out!'

The hooves kept coming at the same pace and she edged Rumbler as far to the side as she could, but it wasn't going to be enough. She started backing up, but horses don't reverse very easily. The oncoming rider came around the bend on a chestnut mare and nearly piled into her. Both horses reared and the other rider tumbled backwards out of his saddle. He hit the ground with a thud, but immediately leapt to his feet, knife in hand. Riadni looked down at him in amusement.

'I hope you're better with a knife than you are with a horse, or you're going to embarrass yourself twice in one day.'

He was a boy, not much older than her, perhaps sixteen, with a mop of brown hair, startling blue eyes and nut-brown skin. He scowled up at her, then his eyes went wide and he laughed.

'Better to be unhorsed than undressed,' he retorted.

Riadni gasped and went bright red beneath the make-up. Her wig! She tried to gather her hair up with one hand as the other pulled her headscarf and wig from the saddle behind her. The boy looked away, embarrassed for her as she fumbled to put them on. He picked up his fallen hat and dusted it off.

'Sorry,' he mumbled, 'I thought you were a boy at first, then ...' He shrugged.

Riadni finished tying her scarf and dropped down out of the saddle to guide Rumbler back down the path out of the boy's way. He held his horse's bridle, talking to it and calming the mare down for a minute, before climbing onto its back.

'Are you one of Elbeth's men?' Riadni asked.

'Who are you?' he asked suspiciously. 'What are you doing out here on your own, anyway?'

'Sostas Mocranen is my father,' she snapped. 'The land below is ours and I can ride wherever I want, on my own or not.'

'Ah, Mister Mocranen,' he nodded. 'They said he had a wildcat for a daughter.'

'Well, "they" should watch their mouths,' Riadni said, getting back into her saddle. 'The last boy to call me names lost a tooth, and he was older than you. Anyway, aren't you a bit young for a freedom fighter?'

'You're never too young to fight,' he muttered, suddenly serious again.

'"You're never too young to fight",' she mimicked, a smile creeping onto her face, 'never too young to scrap with other cowherds and stable boys, sure. But fighting the Altimans – that's different. They'll kill you from a thousand feet in the air. You won't even see their faces.'

'I'll go to their cities. I'll see plenty of faces there,' he said. 'That's what we train for. I'm not ready yet, but when Master Elbeth says I'm ready, then I'll go.'

Riadni wanted to mock his seriousness, but she didn't. He was proud and determined and she found that interesting. He was different from the other boys she knew; he was more than just a farmer's son, or a herdsman; he had purpose.

'And how long will that take?' she asked. 'Should I be

careful riding up to sharp bends for the next few months? Start wearing a helmet?'

'Only if you are going to keep on riding around with your modesty exposed,' he grinned. 'Not that I'm complaining, of course.'

She blushed again.

'I would ... please don't tell anyone about that,' she begged. 'My father would be really upset. The whole village would–'

'I won't tell a soul,' the boy assured her. 'I'll keep your hair to myself. You have my word.'

'How do I know your word is any good?' Riadni sniffed.

'Because,' he smiled as he squeezed past her, their knees brushing against each other for a moment, 'if my riding was as good as my word, I would not have fallen off my horse.'

With that, he touched his heels to the mare's flanks, waved, and galloped off down the trail. Riadni waved back and then realised she had never asked him his name. She made her way home at a slower pace, thinking about the boy and the group that he had given his life to. That evening, for reasons she didn't even want to admit to herself, she asked her mother to make her a new dress.

+ + + +

Benyan Akhna rode into the Hadram Cassal camp in time to see Lakrem Elbeth walk into one of the caves. With a reflexive look up into the sky, he dismounted and led his mare to the corral, which was simply a fenced-off cave that kept the animals out of sight of aircraft. He lifted off the saddle and blanket, unbuckled the bridle and carried them down to his camouflaged tent, which squatted with several others near the three covered lorries under their own camouflage webbing. Only senior members of the group enjoyed the cool, sheltered, but limited space in the caves. He thought about going after Elbeth and telling their leader about his meeting with Mocranen's daughter, but decided against it. He had been ordered to keep away from the farms and villages. Nobody had said anything about bumping into tomboys in the hills. The memory of her lush, deep brown hair framing dark, almond-shaped eyes brought a smile to his face once more. He would dearly love to see that sight again, but chances like that did not come along twice in a lifetime.

A herd of mountain cattle was kept nearby; the youngest members took turns watching over them. Benyan would have his shift this evening. The scrawny, agile cattle served to explain movement around the caves and were particularly useful for covering up the tracks of the horses. It was a pity that their meat tasted like well-worn sandals.

Benyan had been with the Hadram Cassal for a little over six months. He was one of the youngest in this group and was still proving himself to the experienced fighters. Every morning, he and the other recruits ran up into the hills for miles with backpacks full of rocks. He had to learn to load a musket blindfold and shoot from horseback, to fight with his hands and feet, with a knife, sword, belasto and other weapons. He drilled, ran assault courses, tended the horses and the mountain cattle, and in the evenings he and the other recruits had to cook, serve and clean up after meals. The late evening was spent in prayer or reading from one of the three books of Shanna. It was a hard life, but he was growing strong and quick and soon he would take his place among the other fighters. Perhaps he would even have his chance to join the martyrs.

Changing from his riding boots into some soft-soled shoes, he thought again about the girl. He was supposed to have given up any thoughts of life outside the order, but now he could not get her out of his mind. He had to be careful, if he let thoughts of her get under his skin, he would lose his edge. A good warrior had to be able to clear his mind, to fight and kill without compunction.

A year ago, he would not have thought himself capable of any of this. He had been the son of a schoolteacher. He did not hate the Altimans, he even admired them and wanted to go and spend some time in their cities and see how they lived. He wanted to learn their science and maybe even get to fly. He had met few Altimans in his life, and the ones he had met were interesting, well-travelled people.

But a year ago, a factory in his town, run by Altimans, had burned down. The factory had employed over two hundred people, mostly women, including his mother. There had been a lot of accidents there, they made pots and pans and other metal parts and there were huge presses that stamped tin and steel into shapes and people got hands and arms caught and crushed in these machines. Despite constant complaints, nothing was done to make the factory floor safer. The managers did not care; new employees were easy to find in Bartokhrin.

But when people started holding strikes in protest, the plant started to lose money. One day, a fire broke out and the workers could not get out fast enough; there were not enough doors and windows and many of those were locked or barred.

Fifty women died. Benyan's mother was one of them and Benyan and his father were devastated. His father found the managers and told them that he knew about the insurance on the factory and that he could prove the fire had been started deliberately. He wanted them to face up to what they had done and to try and make it right for the people who had been injured and those who had lost loved ones.

When the managers would not listen, Benyan's father went to the Altiman government. Then the managers started listening. His father's body was found in an alleyway in Victovia, the Altiman capital. His family was told that it looked like a mugging that had ended in murder. But the muggers had not taken his father's wristwatch or his rings.

Benyan was an only child and he was brought to live with his aunt and uncle. It was his uncle who talked to him about Bartokhrian history. For centuries, Altima and its enemy, Traucasis, had invaded Bartokhrin from one side and the other, ravaging the country and its people.

Now Bartokhrin had its own government, guided by the Church of Shanna, but was still controlled by Altima and a servant to its trade. Instead of invading armies, they had their land slowly being eaten up by mines and factories owned by faceless men in distant cities. A land starved by other countries of its farmland and raw materials had been reduced to serving those countries like a tramp begging for crusts.

Benyan had listened to their history with a growing hatred and when the godless Altimans flew their planes over his town, delivering destruction to the innocent people who lived there in revenge for the martyrs' attacks on Victovia, sixteen-year-old Benyan Akhna became one of scores of young men joining the order of the Hadram Cassal.

He drove the memory of Mocranen's daughter from his mind. He was a warrior, a servant of Shanna and the order. Crawling out of his tent with his sword, he drew the curved blade from its scabbard and took up a defensive stance. With swift, smooth movements, he practised his exercises in the cooling breeze of the late afternoon. He was a warrior, a servant of Shanna and the order. He needed nothing else in his life.

Seventeen

Worship three times a week, Riadni thought, but only one rest day. It didn't seem a fair trade. She stood in the lines with her mother, and the other women on the left side of the churchground. It was raining, but that did not matter, Monday worship had to be celebrated under an open sky. The men were not allowed to wear their wide-brimmed hats, which would have made sense, but women were permitted bonnets to protect their wigs and face-paint. Like so many her age, Riadni had little respect for the rituals of her religion; most of which seemed unnecessary and some downright daft. The sermon came to an end and the priest, Brother Fazekiel, stepped down from his platform and strode purposefully towards the back of the churchground, a look of thunder on his face.

Riadni looked towards the back and there, standing in the last line of the men's half, were four individuals who must have slipped in after the start of the service. They were dressed in shabby, mud-stained riding clothes and toting pistols in low-slung holsters, which they were trying to hide beneath their hats. Everyone could tell they were from the Hadram Cassal.

'Have you no respect!' the priest roared, as he came up to them. 'Bringing weapons here? You make a lie of everything Shanna teaches us with your violence. Don't bring it into my churchground!'

Fazekiel was an imposing figure, tall and thin, and blessed with a rich, booming voice. He was over sixty years old, but still had sharp, piercing eyes and a vigour that belied his age. The crowd closed in around the men from the Hadram Cassal, knowing a good row brewing when they saw one. Riadni was startled to see that the boy she had run into was one of them. She wished she knew his name. Craning her neck discreetly to get a better view, she wracked her brains to come up with some way to get his attention. This was a difficult proposition, considering girls were not even supposed to make eye contact with men outside their family.

The eldest of the four rebels, a hatchet-faced man with weathered skin and eyes that seemed to have no white to them, raised his hands in a placating gesture to the priest.

'We've just come to worship, Brother. We don't mean any harm.'

'Come to look for more young men to commit mortiphas for your cause, more like,' Fazekiel snorted. 'You do as much harm to the people of this town as you do to the Altimans. Tell Elbeth he's not welcome here, nor anyone else who thinks killing gets things done.'

'Why don't you let the people decide that for themselves?' the other man asked. 'They might have different ideas. We all know where you stand, Brother. You'd try and reason with the enemy. We think they'll take more convincing.'

Riadni listened impatiently. When the service was over, the women were supposed to leave the churchground first, while the men would wait in their positions until it was their turn to go. Outside the gate, the men and women would fall back into their family groups and she might have a short time to talk to the young rebel as the older women stopped to gossip.

'You don't convince anyone of your right to a free existence by convincing them that you threaten theirs,' Fazekiel argued. 'If an Altiman walked into an eating house in Kemsemet and killed everyone there, would we think him a hero with a genuine grievance, or a monster with bloodlust? And why is it only the young men are giving their lives for your cause? Why do we not see Elbeth, or any of his like, committing mortiphas for the Hadram Cassal? Just like the Altimans, your old men send the young ones to do the dying.'

Riadni was sure that if she could let a lock of her hair slip from under her wig just as she passed the row of men at the back, it would seize the attention of every man who saw it, but she would only glance up at one, that would be enough to goad him on. Carefully she slid a finger up under her hairpiece as if scratching an itch, pulling a few strands of her hair free of its pins, but tucking them loosely under the edge of the wig. Her mother cast a suspicious look sideways at her.

'Preach all you like on the churchground, Brother!' one of the other fighters exclaimed. 'But it takes action to get the job done! You can't compare the Altimans with civilised folk. And they don't walk into eating houses; they bomb them from the clouds!'

People started speaking up, some in support of the rebel, others taking the priest's side. Riadni used the disturbance to try and peer over the heads of the congregation. She knew she was being a bit obvious, but she didn't care.

'Riadni!' her mother hissed. 'Behave yourself! What's got into you?'

The hard-faced man who had spoken first marched up to the podium and turned to face the crowd. The other members of the Hadram Cassal followed him.

'How many bombs are we going to let them drop before we do something about it?' he demanded. 'I'm looking for men with the courage to stand up against the forces of oppression and fight for our people's freedom! Men with the courage to show the Altimans that every Bartokhrian life they take will have to be paid for *tenfold!*'

There were cheers from some of the crowd – mostly the men. Riadni was shocked at the way they had upstaged the priest. It was a violation of everything she knew, but she also drew perverse pleasure from seeing the sanctity of their religion cast aside. These men were right in what they were doing. The people needed to be woken up. Fazekiel's peaceful protests and marches were getting nothing done. The Hadram Cassal was taking the fight to the enemy. They had fire in their veins and Riadni felt it too. Up at the podium, Fazekiel was trying to reason with the crowd.

'Would you give the Altimans the excuse they need to send their machines up into our skies? Don't be blind! Don't let these men weaken us by turning us against each other! The Altimans kill us because they think we are animals to be put down, and how can we convince them otherwise when we send assassins to kill their women and children? Shanna will judge us all and murderers will be the first to be cast down!'

'Shanna is with us!' the leader of the rebels cried. 'And it's not murder when you're at war! You can leave our fate in the hands of those who would *talk* our country to death, or you can give your support to the men who will drive the Altimans from our soil for good. The decision is yours!'

There was another cheer of approval. The two factions in the crowd were throwing taunts and insults back and forth and in the midst of it all, Riadni could see the boy with the blue eyes standing proudly with his comrades. The rebels, their job done, filed out between the male and female halves of the congregation. They walked up past her and with a flick of her finger, she let the lock of hair fall across her face, but two bickering women pushed in front of her and the boy did not see. She swore under her breath and could only watch helplessly as the men walked out the gate of the churchground, leaving the seeds of rebellion sprouting behind them in the rain.

✦   ✦   ✦   ✦

Chamus was in the railway room, running the trains around the circuit. The models made enough noise to break the silence in the house, the low hum and soft clattering disturbed the hush and kept the whispering in his head at bay. He wasn't supposed to be there without his grandfather, but it was a Monday and everybody was out. His father and grandfather were at the workshop and his mother was at the office, where she did the accounts for the company, and the housekeeper only worked in the mornings. He was home from school, excused because of a terrorist threat. It had turned out to be a hoax, but they had all been sent home anyway – just to be on the safe side. He often wondered why his school had been targeted all those months ago in the first attacks, but he had been told that the Fringelanders hated the pilots like Commander Ellese, who flew for the Altiman air force. The air-force bases were well guarded, the school's airfield and its budding flyers were not.

As his eyes followed a train around its track, his gaze fell on his grandfather's drawing board in the corner of the big room. He kept it at home for sketching out ideas and there were some sheets of layout paper sitting on the sloped surface. Always interested in seeing the ideas that might someday become real flying machines, Chamus skirted the model railway and sat down at the desk. The drawings were not of an aeroplane, at least not any plane that Chamus had ever seen. It didn't even look like an aeroplane part. It was cylindrical, perhaps part of a bomb, except that there was a section in the middle that, according to the notations, was lined with lead. Lead was the kind of material you avoided on an aircraft. It was too heavy, and weight was a vital concern when designing a machine that had to leave the ground for a living.

He leafed through the half-dozen pages, looking at the different variations and views of the device. There was a scribble that showed the cylinder connecting to a canister of compressed air, which made it look like it was supposed to spray something, a liquid or a powder.

On one page there was a note about dispersal, which

could be about explosives, but then on another, his grandfather had scribbled some chemical formulae and Chamus knew enough about chemistry to know the elements didn't make up nitroglycerine, or any other explosive he had heard of. As far as he and his classmates were concerned, how to make things blow up, dissolve, rot, or otherwise self-destruct was all chemistry was good for. That and making beer, which they had tried once and been violently sick after tasting the results.

There were some photographs lying to one side of the desk and he picked them up. One showed a man wearing a white suit that covered every inch of him, including his head, with a plastic faceplate to allow him to see out. He was holding a small beaker full of what looked like silver-white powder, but Chamus couldn't tell what it was. The other two photos were of a glider that he recognised; it was a craft that his grandfather had designed. This one had been painted black and did not even wear any insignia, as if it was waiting for the paint job to be completed.

There was a sound at the front of the house – the front door opening. Chamus heard his grandfather's voice and hurriedly put the photos and drawings back as he had found them. He rushed to the control box and turned off the model railway, then flicked the light switch off. There he waited in the shadows, preparing his excuse in case his grandfather came in. He did not hear his dad's voice, maybe Grandad had come back early on his own. There was no way to leave the room without walking down the corridor and past the drawing room where his grandfather was.

His ears peeled, he listened intently. He heard two more

voices, but didn't recognise them. Carefully avoiding the creaking floorboard just beyond the door of the room, he crept closer to the drawing room. His grandfather was having a conversation with two other men in the room; Chamus could just make out what was being said.

' … just like to know who's in the loop, that's all,' his grandfather was saying.

'We understand, Thomex, but the whole thing depends on everyone knowing only what they need to know,' said a man with a heavy north-coast accent, 'the less you know about the other members of the group, the better.'

'Besides,' a second man spoke up in a high, reedy voice, 'you want to keep your part in this very quiet. It's only fair to expect everyone else to want the same.'

'That's different, Balan,' Thomex came back. 'Everyone else isn't expected to build the damned thing. My reputation and my life are at risk working with this stuff and the same goes for anyone I bring in to help me. What I want to know is who knows enough to blow the whistle if things get tough.'

'Very few people know of your part in it,' the northern-accented voice said calmly, 'and they are all in powerful positions, untouchable.'

'And you two, of course. Any other well-informed lackeys I should know about?'

'No,' the man named Balan replied tightly, 'just the two lackeys you see before you.'

'A likely story,' Chamus's grandfather retorted. 'These powerful, untouchable people, they do their own typing, do they? Serve their own tea and crumpets? Somebody's always around to take care of the little things and they're the dangerous ones, the ones you don't notice because they're part of the furniture. I'm putting my arse on the line and I don't want to lose it because some toff lets the cat out of the bag giving his secretary dictation, you follow?'

'We hear what you're saying,' Balan reassured him. 'Every possible precaution will be taken. Now, can we get down to the business at hand? Pedrat?'

'Yes,' the northern man piped up. 'We were discussing signs and symptoms. Outside of what only a doctor is going to find in a detailed examination, there will be bleeding from the lips and gums, lesions on the skin, loss of hair and teeth, headaches, nausea, vomiting, diarrhoea …'

'My God,' Thomex gasped. 'How long does it take?'

'The first symptoms show up between a few hours and a few days after you catch it, depending on the strength of the dose. If you survive the initial effects, there can be some damned awful long-term damage. This is pretty nasty stuff. That is why they are going to need our help. That's the whole point.'

'And what if they don't ask us to help them?'

'They'll have to,' Balan said. 'We could see whole villages coming down with this. They're going to need all the help they can get. They'll need our doctors to treat it and the doctors will need the army to contain it, stop it spreading. Even if they don't ask us in, we'll have to insist because of the risk of it being carried up to the plateaux.'

Chamus listened, riveted, to the discussion. So his grandfather was being asked to help deal with the epidemic he had heard about in Bartokhrin. But these men were not medical staff; they were military. Could the terrorists have found a way to carry the disease into the cities? That would explain why his grandfather was being so secretive. He was always going on about security and 'need to know'. Grandad thought the public would panic if they were ever told even half of what the military knew.

'And are we ready to deal with it?' Thomex pressed. 'Do our doctors know how to treat it?'

'We'll be ready to deal with it,' Pedrat answered, 'by the time you've figured out how to get it onto a plane, Thomex. We'd like that to be less than two weeks from now.'

'That's cutting it a bit tight, I don't mind telling you, everything about this thing is experimental. There's going to be some trial and error before we get it right ...'

'We don't have time for messing about, Thomex. There are lives at stake.'

'Don't patronise me, you messenger boy. Don't question my commitment. It'll be ready when it's ready, and that will be when it works and not before. Bloody lackeys. Now sod off out of my house. My grandson is due home soon. And mind you don't slam that door; the coloured glass is delicate.'

Chamus ducked back into the dark as the two men came out. The front door opened and closed, and he waited for a few minutes and listened as his grandfather wheeled himself out of the drawing room and into the kitchen. There was the sound of the kettle being filled and put on a gas ring. It started to heat noisily and Chamus used the sound to close the railway-room door and creep down the corridor. The old man was out of sight behind the kitchen door. Chamus slipped out into the main hallway, opened the front door and closed it again.

'I'm home!' he called. 'Anybody in?'

'In the kitchen, lad!' Thomex called. 'You're back early. Come on in, I'm fixing a brew.'

Chamus joined his grandfather at the kitchen table.

'Can we go and run the trains for a bit?' he asked, because he knew Grandad would expect it of him.

'In a while. I just need to go in and tidy up a little first. There are some private things I need to put away. So, why are you back so early?'

+ + + +

Riadni led Rumbler by the reins over the narrow ridge which ran along the top of Sleeping Hill. She told herself that she was just searching for howler tracks. The bear-sized dogs had been seen over this way and she wanted to be sure that they weren't coming far enough into their land to threaten her father's cattle. A single howler could destroy their herd in a month. That was why she was breaking her promise to her father; that was why she was wandering close to the Hadram Cassal camp.

It had nothing to do with the boy with the blue eyes and the mop of brown hair, whom she had met the week before. Nothing whatsoever. But if she happened to run into him (or if he happened to run into her again), then she wouldn't object to hanging around and talking for a while. Not for the first time, she wondered what his name was ... and whether he was promised to anybody. She shook that thought from her head. Her father had started watching how she behaved around boys and she knew he would be looking for a good match. He might ask her if she liked such and such, or drop hints that what's-his-name was a fine figure of a young man, from a good family, but the choice was not hers to make. Her mother and father would choose for her – for the good of the family. And she would love him and be loyal to him. It could not work any other way.

Riadni wondered again what the blue-eyed boy's name was. The people on the coast had blue eyes and brown hair. He had very little accent and he sounded educated. Perhaps the son of a landowner. She remembered his laugh … and then remembered that she was on the lookout for howlers, not suitors. Tugging impatiently on Rumbler's reins, she walked on along the narrow, stony track. Rumbler followed without complaint.

The edge of the ridge fell away ahead of her and she looped the reins around the stump of a bush. Stooping to avoid being caught against the horizon, she made her way forward, getting lower as she saw a herd of mountain cattle on the flat beneath her. Those were not her father's cattle. There was a boy sitting on a boulder near them, keeping watch. Creeping further forward, she came into view of the camp itself. The caves were right below her and at the foot of the hill was a group of six boys crawling under a net. They scrambled out from underneath it, ran to a high wooden wall and vaulted over, plunging into a pool of water on the other side. They waded out and finished the assault course by attacking six scarecrows with a series of strikes with their knives. Riadni stifled a giggle. It was just like watching her brothers playing war. The boys roared a battle-cry and shook their weapons at the sky. It was all a bit daft.

Then she noticed that the boy she had met in the gully was one of the six. She moved further forward to get a better look. Suddenly a man reared up out of a crevice right in front of her. Riadni stumbled backwards and heard Rumbler whinny. Before she could react, an arm curled around her throat from behind and a knife pricked the back of her neck.

'Who are you?' a voice hissed in her ear.

Riadni was terrified, but she wasn't about to give them the pleasure of seeing it.

'I'm Riadni Mocranen,' she choked. 'You are our guests.'

'Bring her to Elbeth,' the one in front of her said. 'He'll have to decide.'

She bit the side of her mouth. Decide what?

As the first one pulled her arms behind her and tied them at the elbows, the other went to fetch Rumbler. Riadni decided to let him. There was a shriek and she and her captor spun around. The second man was lying on the ground holding a hand that was bleeding profusely.

'Oh, I should have told you,' Riadni said flatly. 'He bites.'

'Leave the horse,' the first man snapped. 'Come on.'

The wounded man got to his feet, wrapped a rag around his hand and followed Riadni and her captor down the trail. She got a chance to look at them more carefully. They were dressed in working clothes – canvas trousers, cotton lace-up tops and wide-brimmed hats. They wore soft leather boots with thin soles for quiet movement and each had a leather belt with a knife, flintlock pistol in a holster and pouches for powder and ball. She had no doubt they could use both weapons well. Trying to run was out of the question. Besides, the man with the mangled hand was giving her nasty looks and she didn't want to give him any excuses to get his own back.

They marched down into the camp, attracting some attention from the others there. The boy Riadni knew came up to them, walking alongside her.

'You've caught a live one there, Misho,' he said to the man leading her, 'but I don't think you're going to get to keep her. That's Mocranen's daughter you've got there.'

'That's Mister Mocranen to you peasants,' she scowled.

'That's Mister Mocranen's daughter you've got there,' the young man repeated happily. 'Welcome to our humble caves, Miss Mocranen.'

'They're our caves.'

'Welcome to your humble caves, Miss Mocranen.'

She suppressed a smile as Misho waved the boy away. She was led into the mouth of the largest cave, where some older men were hunkered down around a map. They looked up and a few of them smiled. Lakrem Elbeth stood up and beamed at her.

'Miss Mocranen, you bless us with your presence. But I don't think your father will be very happy. I'm sure he told you what a bad influence we are. Or perhaps that is the very reason you went against his wishes?' He spread his hands. 'Tea?'

'Sorry?' she frowned. 'Oh. No, thank you. I should be getting home now. If you'd untie me …'

'But you've only just arrived. I'm sure you're curious about what we do here.'

He motioned with his hand and Misho quickly untied her arms.

Riadni stared at him. The only advantage of wearing Shanneyan make-up was that it made her feelings harder to read. Elbeth's expression had a mask all its own, but she did not see the welcome there that his words offered. She had broken a promise to come here, had been caught spying on a place that was supposed to be secret. She knew he was weighing all this up and wondered with sudden fear if the decision that the two lookouts had spoken about, Elbeth's decision, was whether or not she was to be killed.

'My father will be asking where I am.'

'I'm sure he asks that all the time,' Elbeth shrugged. 'He is a devout man, and you are not exactly an ideal Shanneyan daughter. It is still early. Misho, where is the lady's horse?'

'Up on the hill. It bit Carlec's hand, so we left it.'

Everyone turned to look at Carlec, who was standing to attention with his ragged bandage dripping blood.

'It nearly took off my fingers, Master Elbeth,' he blurted out, cradling his hand.

'Which would have no doubt halved your mathematical abilities,' Elbeth muttered. 'Have Jasker see to your wound. Misho, leave the horse where it is for now, but return to your post. Miss Mocranen … may I call you Riadni?'

Riadni was stumped. As a friend of her father's, he was entitled to call her by her first name. As an older man she had met only once before, he was required to be more formal. Most men were, until they were told otherwise.

'No,' she said, 'Miss Mocranen, if you don't mind.'

'Of course. Well Miss Mocranen, I couldn't help noticing that young Akhna recognised you when you walked in. You've met before?'

She hesitated. She hadn't realised he had watched them walk through the camp.

'I've seen him. I didn't know his name.'

'His name is Benyan Akhna,' Elbeth gazed out at the boys practising stick-fighting, 'a fine figure of a young man. We expect great things from him. Perhaps you'd like to fetch your horse and join his group for some riding exercises?'

Riadni blinked. Perhaps she would.

 Sixteen

For Chamus, it was like being back on that taxiway – scraped, battered and barely conscious. The sound could still be heard from a few streets away, even though the sireniser was already winding down. It must be one of the Haunted, he thought. Another insane Fringelander committing mortiphas for his 'cause'. We shouldn't even be able to get this close without ear protectors, and a real sireniser goes on for hours.

He was with his classmates, on their way to the war museum on a school trip. Their tram had been stopped, along with all the other traffic, by police, half a mile from the old building. Then suddenly they had heard it. Crisp, but heavy and mournful, the sound of a sireniser going off. There was the split of concrete and the shattering of glass as every window near the blast blew out. Everyone in the tram covered their ears, except Chamus. He knew that if the sound was going to hurt them, it would have already. A cloud of dust rolled down the street towards them, most of it thinning out and dispersing before it hit them.

'Here, Constable,' Vel Sillian called to one of the

policemen, 'what did they hit?'

'The war museum,' the copper replied. 'The nutter stood there chanting for nearly ten minutes. Looked like he was having an argument with himself, apparently. Seems like the bad half won the toss. Still, we had time to get most of the people out.'

Most of the people, Chamus thought. Wonder how many that left?

'Trip's over then, Miss?' Sillian turned to their history teacher, Mrs Archaw.

'Sit down, please, Sillian, until the police tell us whether or not we can go.' Mrs Archaw was a plump, jovial woman, but there were tears in her eyes now and a quiver in her voice.

'Oh, you can take the youngsters away, Miss,' the policeman nodded, 'no need for them to hang around. Only adding to the noise if you know what I mean.'

'Only too well, Constable,' she said shakily. 'Right, all of you, there's no sense sitting in all this traffic. Out you get and start walking. That means you too, Roddins. Don't make me say it twice.'

There was some moaning from the class, but Chamus was glad for the chance to walk. The other girls and boys were talking excitedly and even he was caught up in the atmosphere. All around them, people were getting out of their vehicles and talking about the attack. People in the street never talked to each other, but today they all had something in common, he realised. Today, someone was trying to kill them. The terrorists picked on ordinary folks, not soldiers or politicians; the attacks were aimed at anybody who lived in Victovia or any of the other half-dozen major cities in Altima.

You didn't have to be fighting against the Fringelanders; you just had to be one of a few million people living in the wrong place.

This was one of the oldest parts of town, right in the centre of the city. The buildings were ornate and permanent, made of sandstone and granite, with tall windows, high ceilings and proud workmanship. The streets were cobbled and the kerbs high, from the days when horse-drawn carriages were still used. That would have been almost two centuries ago, Chamus thought to himself; the first powered flight had happened back then, when even motorcars were still in their infancy. Man had ruled the skies for nearly a hundred and fifty years and there was still so much room up there to explore.

He looked up into the sky. The dust was joining the smog, blocking out the blue he loved. Police balloons hung at regular points across the city, anchored to the tallest buildings, the overcoated constables watching over the inhabitants with binoculars. As always, at least one or two other aircraft could be seen under the low, scattered clouds. Sillian caught him staring skywards and punched him on the shoulder.

'Do you ever think about anything else, Cham?' he asked. 'When are you going to start staring at girls like that?'

'When they grow wings and a propeller,' Chamus smiled back.

'Now we know why your canopy gets all steamed up during flying lessons,' Sillian chortled. 'Oi! Cham's never taking the rear seat in my bird again!'

There was a cackle from the other boys, and Roddins

grabbed his crotch with one hand and stuck the other out like a wing, buzzing from side to side with an engine sound.

'Demonstrating poor use of your joystick there, Roddins,' Sillian barked, like their flying instructors. 'Ride the plane. Don't let her ride you.'

'Sillian!' Mrs Archaw snapped from the front, looking around. 'Don't think I can't hear you!'

'Yes, Miss,' the dark-haired boy answered dutifully. 'Tell us some history, Miss.'

'Well I'm glad you asked, Sillian. This is the perfect opportunity.'

'Arse-licker,' Chamus whispered. 'We were going to miss class.'

'We still will,' Sillian muttered back. 'She can't hear a thing over the sound of her own voice.'

'You'd be surprised what I can hear over the sound of my own voice. Now pipe down.'

The two boys paid great attention to their feet.

'This is the perfect opportunity to cover some Fringelands' history. It might put today's events in some perspective,' Mrs Archaw began, and the whole class sighed silently. They could tell when she was preparing for one of her lengthy lectures. 'There are four Fringeland nations bordering the Altiman plateaux: Majarak, Bartokhrin, Constantin and Nathelem. Each claims to be a democratic republic, although Majarak is currently ruled by a dictator who seized power with the army two years ago, and Nathelem has had seven governments in three years because of various *coups* and scandals.

'Altima and Traucasis fought a number of wars for the

domination of the valuable resources in these lands.'

'Where did they fight the wars, Miss?' Chamus asked. They didn't often do Fringelands' history, and it sounded like they might be missing out on some gory stories.

'Well, normally in the land that was the subject of the dispute, Chamus. That is the tradition with wars. Now, Majarak was the first to win its independence, forming its first political party late in the last century ...'

And so it went on. Like so many history lessons, it was a collection of political facts, dates and places. Chamus wished they could hear more of the stories – especially the war stories. He thought about why they were walking back to school. Their school trip had been cancelled because people had been killed and all they were worried about was not getting back in time for their afternoon classes.

'Why do they hate us, Miss?' he asked suddenly.

'They don't all hate us,' she said slowly, 'but the problem is that the ones who do are the ones we see and hear. It's like being in a room full of strangers, who all look similar and most of whom talk quietly. But there's one who wants to shout all the time. The others have things to say, if only you would listen to them, but you only listen to the man who shouts, because his behaviour has your attention. Violent behaviour gets our attention.'

'So are the men who come to Altima to kill people ... are they just nuts?' Sillian asked.

'A few of them are, I suppose,' Mrs Archaw tilted her head, 'but most of them start out as normal people and the things that happen to them make them so frustrated that they become fanatics. Most people become fanatical for a reason.

'Some claim that they are avenging a history of oppression, torture ... the kinds of crimes every conquering country carries out as a matter of course in the race for power. But I can tell you as a history teacher, that most people don't care about history unless they can relate what happened in the past to what is happening now. If people suffered in the past, but their descendants are content with their lives now, the descendants aren't likely to go out and kill in the name of history. But if people are suffering the same harsh treatment *now* that their parents and grandparents and great-grandparents went through, then you have generations of discontentment coming to the boil.

'Yes, I think what it comes down to in the end is a lack of contentment.'

The students looked at one another with expressions of puzzlement and scorn. 'Lack of contentment' didn't make someone into a terrorist. Chamus remembered the day at the hangar, when his class died, and when he returned later to see the bodies being pulled out. Hate coursed through him every time he thought about it and he wanted to hurt the people who had carried it out, except the only one he knew about was dead. He would wake up in the morning and the whispering would come to him in the last quiet moments of sleep, reminding him of what had happened, and he would find his hands clawing the sheets and his teeth grinding with the hate. That was the kind of thing that made a person into a killer. Lack of contentment was going around with a bad haircut.

'I think you're wrong, Miss,' he pronounced, in a flat tone.

Mrs Archaw regarded him for a moment, and then gazed

around her as if admiring the architecture.

'Has anybody heard of a man named Olam Waymath?'

Nobody answered; the name meant nothing to them. Which was a sure sign they were in for a lecture.

'I think you'll recognise him when I tell you his story. Olam Waymath was born in Bartokhrin, in a region called Gefinlan,' the teacher began, and the class listened resignedly in expectation of another list of dates and places. But Mrs Archaw did not start reciting historical data. 'Olam was the son of a fisherman, and grew up in a relatively peaceful village. He was much the same as any of you, without the benefits of your exceptional education, of course.

'That was until he turned thirteen. On his thirteenth birthday, the local councillor came to the village and told the people there that their river was to be blessed with the protection of a hydroelectric dam, which was to be built upstream. Olam and all the other boys watched over the months that followed as the rich men of Bartokhrin brought in Altiman engineers and construction teams to put up this huge dam that formed a new horizon above their village. The rich men were buying up plots of land along the valley, and Olam's father sold some land near his house for an excellent price and got ready to welcome some wealthy neighbours.

'But the dam did not turn out to be the blessing the councillors had claimed. Pylons were erected on the newly bought plots of land, making the area look like a massive power station. The construction ruined a large section of the valley and when the dam became operational, the river flowing through the village dried up. Fish eggs didn't hatch and rice didn't grow, because the flood plains didn't get flooded. Olam and his family went hungry – along with most of their friends and neighbours. With no fish or rice, half the people in the village lost their livelihood. To add insult to injury, it turned out the village was to get none of the electricity that was to come from the dam. It went over their heads through the pylons and on to the rich towns in Nathelem and Altima, and the councillors who were supposed to look after the area had been bribed into submission long ago.

'Olam watched his family descend into poverty and starvation over the next three years; he watched his two sisters die of diseases the family couldn't afford to treat and saw his family thrown out of their home as debtors seized their land. Olam had joined in the protests when this had all started. He had helped sabotage pylons and power substations when protesting failed. Because of the sabotage, Bartokhrin sent in Altiman-trained troops to provide security for the pylons. That was like a red rag to a bull as far as the villagers were concerned and their operations went from sabotage to all-out guerrilla warfare. Olam was one of these fighters, dedicated and deadly, and he ended up being persuaded by the leaders of this resistance to take on a terrifying mission, one he carried out with spectacular success, but at the cost of his own life.

'The people of Gefinlan are still living their lives surrounded by soldiers who hate and abuse them. They are held in contempt all over Bartokhrin, and their valley has become a burned and ruined landscape as both sides continue to ravage each other. The pylons have long stopped providing any electricity. The whole conflict started because of the greed of a few people on either side, but now both sides hate each other so much, the fighting has become its own justification. And the people sing songs about killers like Olam.'

'But that's not lack of contentment, Miss,' Chamus spoke up. 'That's somebody walking all over you and then demanding you lick your blood off their shoes. The villagers couldn't just sit there and take it.'

'And they didn't,' their teacher said, 'but the government found itself dealing with terrorists and answered force with force by sending in the army. But now what's the answer? Bartokhrin cannot give in to murderers and terrorists, because that would be saying that anyone who wants to commit enough murder will eventually get their own way, which would lead to much more violence in the long run. But the "freedom fighters" won't stop killing because it is the only way they can see of getting an occupying army out of their valley. So you have a situation where neither side can back down. And even if they stopped fighting and the villagers were allowed to go back to their way of life, would that guarantee peace?'

'No,' said Chamus, 'because they'd still hate all the people who caused their problems. And they'd still be living in a country that hated them.'

'Yes,' Mrs Archaw nodded. 'Perhaps if everyone concerned managed to tolerate each other for a few generations, when people had got over the bad feelings, they might forgive and forget. But only if there no other problems that they could blame on each other. Only if they were content.'

'I still don't know who Olam Waymath was,' Sillian spoke

up, feeling they were getting off the point.

'He was known here under the name he adopted when he came to Victovia,' Mrs Archaw told them. 'Here, his name was Jered Wyman.'

Everyone looked reflexively at Chamus. He stared straight ahead and avoided their eyes, a bitter expression on his face.

Jered Wyman was the name of the madman who had killed his class.

The class was quiet as they strolled along the road to their school. Mrs Archaw looked at her watch.

'I see you're going to be on time for Mr Morthrom's class ... that's of course unless you have more questions. In which case, I think we could stretch our little walk out a bit longer, do another lap around the block. So, any more questions?'

A dozen hands shot into the air. She clasped her hands together.

'It's amazing how a bit of fresh air can stimulate one's brain.'

 # Fifteen

Riadni's father had never shown her how to use a gun. Girls did not use guns, after all. Up until now, she had had no idea there were so many things that could go wrong.

'You have to tamp the powder right down,' Benyan was saying, 'and then the ball must fit tightly up against it. Any space between it and the powder will allow gases to expand inside the barrel and it could explode on you. Don't let the barrel drop towards the ground as you aim, and if it doesn't fire when you pull the trigger, point it in a safe direction for a minute in case the powder is burning slowly. It might still fire.'

They were on the firing range and Benyan was instructing her in the use of a flintlock pistol. There was so much to remember: clean the barrel constantly, keep the powder dry, how to load and how to avoid a misfire … She noticed that the more senior members of the order carried revolvers and bolt-action rifles – modern weapons captured from Altimans and coveted by the veteran fighters. But all the young recruits learned on the older weapons.

'Now,' Benyan continued, 'hold it at arm's length, crook your elbow a little to take the shock … that's it. It'll kick when it fires. Look down the barrel, line up the sights and squeeze slowly …'

His hand held her arm as he guided her movements and she wondered if he was aware of what he was doing. Lakrem Elbeth watched from behind them and she knew he must be noting this forbidden contact. He seemed to be taking a personal interest in her introduction to their training.

She squeezed off a shot and her arm jolted with the shock. The sound nearly deafened her. She looked through the smoke at the circular target. She was wide of the mark, but at least she had hit the board.

'Nice shot,' Benyan nodded. 'You could be good at this, you know.'

There was a warmth in his voice and he kept looking at her and then averting his gaze. Riadni smiled and self-consciously adjusted her wig. Her arm hurt from the recoil of the gun, but she didn't care, she was having the time of her life. They had started with horsemanship and she had managed to match the boys move for move. Elbeth had been impressed and suggested that she try some shooting. He had partnered her with Benyan and soon she had completely lost track of time. While he taught her, the boy had talked to her about his parents and why he had joined the Hadram Cassal. Listening to his story, she imagined what she would have done if someone had killed her parents – probably exactly as he had done.

Handling the hot barrel carefully, she started the process

of reloading the pistol. Elbeth approached them and with a motion with his hand dismissed Benyan, who bowed and stood back.

'We can continue your lesson another time,' Elbeth told her, 'but it is getting late and your father will be starting to worry. I think it would be best if you didn't tell him you were here. He wouldn't take it well.'

Riadni nodded and put the pistol down on the table beside her. Looking up at the evening sky, she realised how late she was. Her parents would be furious. She had missed supper.

'You are welcome to come back,' said Elbeth, 'but next time, don't be afraid to just ask to see me. I will always have time for the daughter of such a good friend. And such a fine rider too! I think Bartokhrin could use more girls like you.'

Riadni thanked him and turned away quickly to hide her flushed face. It was rare that adults showed any kind of appreciation of her. She turned back to bow briefly and say goodbye and then rushed to her horse, which was corralled with the others in a cave. She led Rumbler out, swung up into the saddle and nudged him into a canter. Benyan and Elbeth waved to her as she passed and then she was riding on past the herd of mountain cattle and into the grassland that stretched out over her route home. Rumbler was tired from the afternoon's training, but he kept up a steady pace across the flat grass and it wasn't long before her house came into sight. Two of her brothers were laying tobacco leaves out to dry in the yard and they looked up as she rode in.

'Papa wants to see you,' Barra told her. 'He's not happy. You were out at the camp, weren't you?'

Riadni said nothing. She unsaddled Rumbler and led him into the corral at the end of the yard, before making her way into the house. Her parents were in the kitchen, sitting at the table with cups of tea. Her mother did not say anything, leaving her father to stand up and face her. That was always a bad sign.

'Where were you?' he asked, his voice trembling slightly.

'Just out for a ride,' she answered. 'I went up by Prospectors' Pass to look for howler tracks ...'

Her father slapped her hard across the head. She put her hand to the side of her face in shock. He had never hit her that hard before.

'If you want to be a boy so much,' he barked, 'then I'll treat you like a boy! You were out at Elbeth's camp, weren't you?'

Riadni stared at her father through watering eyes. She didn't say anything, knowing her voice would crack and then she would definitely cry. She hung her head. Glancing at her mother, she saw a fearful expression on her face and turning her gaze back to her father, saw the same fear behind the anger in his eyes. They were afraid for her.

'Answer me, girl,' he growled. 'I can smell gun smoke on your clothes, by Shanna! What, have they been letting you use a pistol, letting you join in their games? Are they adding little girls to their ranks now?'

'I'm not a little girl!' she snapped.

He hit her again, harder, and this time she did start crying.

'Go out to the yard and help your brothers. Convince me you can do something useful,' Sostas hissed. 'You're not fit to marry. No man will have you. So, Shanna forgive me, we'll just have to make a servant out of you.'

'Sostas!' his wife protested. 'Don't talk to her like that …'

'Don't take her side!' he roared. 'We've been too soft on her and this is what we get! Get outside, girl, and get to work before I have to take my belt to you!'

Riadni stood where she was, her body wracked with sobs. He had never treated her like this before. She could only stand and cry. Her father stood in front of her for a while, then shook his head and left the kitchen. Her mother looked forlornly at her, but she would not go against her husband. After sitting there lost for words for a few minutes, she left too and Riadni hung her head back and cried at the ceiling.

✦   ✦   ✦   ✦

Benyan was too wound up to sleep. Instead, he tried to read the Parrelam, the second book of Shanna, but he could not keep his mind on it. The passage was about the appreciation of beauty and the evidence of the existence of the she-god wherever beauty was to be seen. The appreciation of beauty was a gift given only to man, of all Shanna's creations. No animal could see the world as man saw it, for it was only man who had been created in the image of Shanna. The beauty of women was the ultimate example of this, and so women were to be protected and kept pure of sin. It was a passage whose poetry was cherished by all who read it, but Benyan could not keep his mind off Riadni Mocranen.

He put the book down and stared out of a gap in the door of the tent he shared with another novice. The words of Lakrem Elbeth came to him; he must focus his mind on what was important, he must think of the cause at all times.

Everything he did, from his training and his chores, to his nightly prayers, must be for the good of the cause. It was hard to see where Riadni fit in, but Master Elbeth seemed to think she had a part to play. Benyan wondered if she would join the struggle and the thought of it gave him a flush of excitement. There was a scratch of fingernails on the door of the tent.

'Benyan? Are you there?' a soft voice called into the tent.

He leaned his head out and saw his tent-mate, Cosca, standing there.

'Master Elbeth wants to see you. He's got all the elders in there too,' the older boy told him. He hesitated, then added, 'They said to bring all your stuff.'

Benyan shared a look with his friend and nodded. They had heard that order given before and knew it could only mean one thing. His hands shook as he pulled on his boots and packed his few personal belongings into his bag. He scrambled out of the tent and stood up, straightened his tunic, put his hat on his head and raised his eyebrows expectantly at Cosca.

'You look fine,' the other boy said. 'Go on, they're waiting!'

Cosca took his hand and clasped it tightly before pushing him towards the caves.

There were five elders, including the leader, sitting in a semicircle with Lakrem Elbeth in the middle. Benyan was taken aback to find he was the only other one to arrive in the cave. He looked back self-consciously, but Elbeth waved to him.

'There will be no one else joining us, Benyan,' he said. 'Please sit down.'

There was a low seat in front of him, like those that the elders sat upon. He sat down carefully. This was a new honour and he wondered what he had done to deserve it … or what he would have to do.

'You have come a long way since you joined us, Benyan,' Elbeth began. 'You have grown, climbed the treacherous steps between boyhood and maturity. We think it is time you took your place among our soldiers.'

Benyan could not keep the smile from his face. His breathing shuddered with pride and happiness. It was the moment he had been waiting for, for nearly a year.

'I am your servant, Master Elbeth.'

'There is one final test. This is the final step to becoming a man, Benyan. An act of cunning, determination and strength. Success will carve your place among the Hadram Cassal.'

Benyan nodded. He was ready. Whatever they asked. He was ready.

'You will go to the city of Victovia,' Elbeth told him as the other elders watched him impassively, 'where you will kill two men and a boy.'

He held out a photograph, crumpled and with peeling edges. It was a picture of two men, one quite old, and a boy who might be around his age. They were standing in front of an aeroplane, a fighter with a huge engine in its nose and machine guns mounted on its single set of wings.

'They are three generations of the same family,' said Elbeth. 'The old man is the most important target; his son and grandson share his home and must die with him. The old man is an engineer who has built a number of the aircraft and weapons that are used to kill our people. His son also practises his accursed trade. The boy must pay for the sins of his father and grandfather. You will be given the Blessing of the Martyrs for this task; they shall lend their guidance and power.'

Benyan bowed his head. The mission was a great honour and he was staggered that he was to receive the Blessing of the Martyrs. It was given only to truly dedicated members of the order. In the back of his mind, a disloyal voice reminded him that it was also only given to men who committed mortiphas, and ended up dying to complete their mission.

'What are their names, Master?'

'They are called Thomex, Kellen and Chamus Aranson.'

FOURTEEN

In the chilly darkness before dawn, Riadni rinsed the sleepiness from her face with cool water from the well bucket. She was sure she had packed everything she needed, but was reluctant to leave in case she had forgotten something. She had never run away before and she was not about to leave now and come back because she had gone without her water bottle or a spare pair of shoes. This had to be for good. A sudden thought occurred to her and she crept back into the house, running her fingers along the familiar adobe walls as she climbed the stairs to her room. She would bring the new dress her mother had laid out on the bed for her. The thought of her mother nearly made her cry. Mama would be heartbroken. Riadni held the dress up and admired the fine fabric and her mother's delicate needlework once more. She wanted Benyan to see her in that dress. Folding it carefully, she put it in her satchel, and then slipped out of the room and down the stairs.

At the bottom of the stairs was the cupboard where her father kept the family's guns. In a moment of sheer nerve, Riadni found the hidden key, opened the locked doors and pulled a flintlock pistol from its mountings. There was a bag of ammunition and a horn full of powder with the gun and she put all three in her bag. If she were to join the Hadram Cassal, she would need her own weapon.

Rumbler was waiting for her outside, his saddlebags already full to bursting. She tied her satchel on top of the bags and looked around her, wondering if there was anything else she had forgotten. The horse stood watching her, his breathing and the shifting of his hooves against the ground the only sounds in the quiet yard. Riadni hesitated, half wishing someone would come out and catch her before she could go, persuade her that there was still something worth staying for. Then she remembered her father's last words to her and she took hold of Rumbler's reins and led him as silently as she could from the yard, out and down the road, until she was sure nobody would hear.

Bringing Rumbler to a halt, she put her foot in its stirrup, vaulted into the saddle and set him off down the road at a steady trot. Her father and brothers would track her, she was sure of that, and they would expect her to make straight for the Hadram Cassal camp. Instead, she headed west, the opposite direction, and lost the horse's tracks in the dust of the busy main road. Where the road forded the river, she turned into the shallow water and waded upstream, coming out into the grassland that swept up towards the mountains and the flat, square shape of Sleeping Hill. She would take a route that would lead her far from her family's farm. It was still dark in the early morning, but she would make sure it took her most of the day to reach the camp that was to be her new home.

+ + + +

The five elders led Benyan Akhna up the face of a steep slope in almost total darkness. It was a hard climb. He was the youngest by decades, and yet he found it hard to keep up. Sometimes he could only follow by listening when they disappeared into the darkness above him. Eventually, he came out on the top of the hill and found them waiting, standing in a semicircle to receive him. Lakrem Elbeth held a mask in his hands, carved entirely from a single piece of stone. There were no holes for nose or mouth, but in the place of eyes, there were two purple pieces of crystal, glinting in the dim light of the half-moon.

'Pray with us, Benyan,' Elbeth said, and they all turned towards the east.

All six knelt, bowed their heads and covered their eyes, each becoming deeply immersed in his own prayer. They stayed that way until the sky brightened with the dawn and the first glimpse of the sun showed over the ragged edge of the horizon.

'Now we will begin,' the Hadram Cassal leader told the boy. 'The ceremony will take some time and there will be times when you will feel fear and doubt. Put these from your mind and welcome the power of the martyrs into your soul. These are your personal belongings?'

Benyan nodded and handed over his bag.

'You will change your clothes too. Take off your old things and Jasker here will give you a new set.'

Undressing while the old men turned away to respect his modesty, he pulled on the Altiman-style underwear, vest, slacks and shoes that they gave him. Jasker, the smallest of the elders, had started a fire with some kindling and sacrificial oil and now he threw Benyan's things on it one by one. His mother's silk scarf, his father's prized wristwatch, even his Shanneyan books, Benyan watched numbly as all his most precious possessions were tossed into the flames. It was as if his whole life were being wiped away. While the fire burned, the other men sat him down and groomed him for the task ahead. They trimmed his hair, cleaned and clipped his nails and scrubbed the exposed skin of his neck and hands with a pumice stone. The cloth used to wipe off the rubbed skin was thrown into the fire along with the hair and nail clippings. Then, he was handed a shirt, which he pulled on and buttoned up with trembling fingers. Elbeth looked him up and down and nodded to himself.

'You are ready.'

He motioned to Benyan to lie down on a short slope facing the sunrise and the men crouched around him. Jasker had taken some ashes from the fire and mixed them in a small bowl with some of the sacrificial oil. Elbeth knelt by his head, taking some of the mixture on his fingers, drew lines on Benyan's face, each line tracing a path from the edges of his face in towards his eyes. When this was done, Elbeth wiped his hands and picked up the stone mask, which he laid over Benyan's face. Benyan suffered a moment of claustrophobia as he felt his face covered. Then the first rays of the sun shone through the purple crystals into his eyes. He could hear the men chanting a prayer in a language he did not understand, but one he recognised from the ancient teachings his father had practised. It was comforting to hear the old sounds again.

Then something streamed down the path of the sunlight and into his eyes. He went rigid with shock as shrieks filled his head. He tried to pull the mask away, but the elders were holding his arms and legs, and Elbeth was pressing the cold stone ever harder against his face, gripping the sides of his head. Memories of pain and torture that were not his swept through him. He screamed and thrashed, but the men were strong and held him fast. As fear crushed the breath out of him, he thought of Riadni and how she had made him think of a life beyond the Hadram Cassal and the shrieks grew louder and the pain more intense. The purple light was carrying something with it, as if it were pulling something alive from the bright sky and injecting it into his being. Suddenly he had a feeling of falling backwards, and of other minds filling the space between himself and his senses. They flooded into him and around him and embraced him and it felt good to be part of them. Shanna was offering him glory and heaven the spirits told him. He could join them in paradise once he had completed one small task. He laughed and welcomed them, throwing off the cares that had weighed heavy on him all his life. He was ready to do whatever they asked. No price was too great for the chance to serve Shanna. Nothing would stop him from joining her in paradise.

+ + + +

Benyan was sprawled on the ground and the sun was high in the sky when he awoke. He squinted up at it, realising the mask was gone from his face. Stretching his limbs, he found an energy and strength that he had never known before. There were other minds entwined with his and he felt them move in time with him, as if his body and that of another shared the same space. Elbeth sat cross-legged before him. Benyan sprang to his feet and stood to attention. Elbeth smiled up at him.

'You have the Blessing of the Martyrs upon you,' he said softly. 'Now it is time for you to begin your task. You have memorised the photograph of Thomex Aranson. You will go to his home in Victovia. You will wait until his son and grandson are there with him and you will kill them all. There are men at the bottom of the hill, waiting to take you to the border of Altima. They have all the other things that you will need. Are you ready Benyan Akhna?'

'Yes, Master.'

Elbeth stood up and clasped the boy's hands between his. Benyan felt caught in the man's gaze like prey that had locked eyes with its hunter. His eyes dropped submissively as he bowed to his leader. In the silence between them, he could hear the voices of the dead, whispering promises and prayers and uttering curses on their enemies … and he knew he would be their servant until he took his place with them in paradise.

+ + + +

Chamus sat in the back of the car, gazing out at the barges on the canal, their diesel motors farting smoke out of their sterns, the exhausts puffing in time with the water spat from the engines' cooling systems. It was half-past five on a Saturday, the sun had barely risen, and yet they were stuck in traffic. They were on their way to the airfield where Aranson Air had its base, his mother accompanying his father out to a test flight, Chamus on his way to do some flying in his own plane. He was itching to get to the airfield, but the traffic jam wasn't going anywhere. They had caught up on a column of military vehicles going in the same direction along the canal road and there seemed to be a glut of traffic all the way to the aerodrome. The airfield was situated near one of the major ramps down off the Victovia plateau into Bartokhrin, and Chamus was willing to bet that this was where they were all heading.

'Honestly,' his mother griped, 'I've never seen anything like it. What can they be doing with all these trucks?'

'Something to do with tackling the Hadram Cassal, I'd wager,' Kellen replied, his elbow leaning on the sill of his open window. 'Can't see them moving all this lot into the Fringelands without causing a fuss, though.'

Chamus rolled his eyes. Typical of his father to refer to a possible war as 'a fuss'. It often seemed to Chamus that his father lived in slow motion when he wasn't flying. He was unhurried and infuriatingly careful in everything he did. He was not impatient as they waited for the traffic to get moving, because he had left an hour spare to reach the airfield and get ready. The prototype, high-altitude reconnaissance plane would be prepped and waiting for him when he got there; it certainly wasn't going anywhere without him. To his son's amazement, Kellen turned off the ignition and leaned back in his seat, arms behind his head. His wife, Nita, opened her bag and took out a book on gardening, turning the pages slowly as she enjoyed the practical tips on how to deal with greenfly. Chamus flopped back in the seat and moaned. Nita peered round at him, giving him that look that she had, over the top of her glasses.

'The sky will still be there when you get to the airfield, Cham,' she said to him. 'If you're tired of being cooped up in the car, you could always go for a walk up the canal. I don't think we'll be moving for a while.'

'I could walk all the way and be there before you at this rate.'

'Why don't I come with you, then, and we'll do just that. Your father can catch up. Kellen?'

Kellen nodded and waved at them to go ahead. He turned on the radio and found his favourite jazz station. There weren't many cars around with radios, and he jumped at the chance to use it whenever he could. He turned it up, so that the soldiers in the trucks around them could listen with envy. A lively, big-band number followed Chamus and his mother down the road.

There were a lot of medical services trucks – with the big red cross in a white circle marked over their olive drab paintwork – more than a normal army column would have warranted, but there were also half-tracks, armoured troop carriers and jeeps too. There must have been two hundred vehicles on that section of the road.

'It's as if they're getting ready for a disaster,' Nita muttered. 'I wonder if they've heard about some huge terrorist threat.'

'I don't know,' Chamus thought aloud, remembering the mysterious conversation between his grandfather and the two men. 'I think they're heading out to the Fringelands. Couldn't they just be looking for the terrorists?'

'Bartokhrin's not about to let all this in,' his mother shook her head. 'They've reacted badly enough to our bombers' strikes. If this is seen coming down the ramp, there'll be uproar. No, it's got to be for some kind of emergency, I think. But don't ask me what.'

'Hey, mister!' Chamus called up to one of the soldiers in the back of a covered lorry. 'Where are you going?'

'Just setting up base at the aerodrome, lad,' the man shouted back. 'Providing support for the medics, that's all we know. They don't tell us much, and we can tell even less.'

'Let's walk faster, Mum,' Chamus said, 'the more of these lads that show up, the less room I'm going to have to take off.'

It took half an hour to reach the airfield and when they did, they found vehicles filing in through the security gate, one by one. Chamus and Nita showed their passes, shared a few words with the policeman on guard, whom they knew well, and walked through, making their way to the group of hangars owned by Aranson Air. Thomex was already there, with some of his design engineers. The aircraft that Kellen was to fly sat just inside the open door of the biggest hangar. Outside the smallest, Chamus's plane was being given the once-over by a mechanic.

'Where is he, then?' Thomex asked Nita.

'Lost amongst some trucks, a couple of miles behind us,' she answered. 'What's going on, Thomex? Do you know?'

'Bloody army,' he scowled, as if that was all the explanation she needed.

She regarded the sleek scout plane that sat with its canopy open, awaiting its pilot. The air force was poised to buy the design if the test went well, which would mean big things for their small company.

'It's an insidious-looking thing,' she said, nodding at it.

'What's the weather report like?'

'Excellent,' Thomex spun his wheelchair around to look down the airstrip. 'Wind is five knots at the most. Visibility is near perfect and we're expecting clear skies all afternoon.'

He turned to Chamus: 'Your bird's ready if you want to take her up, Cham.'

'I'll wait for Dad. I want to see him take off,' Chamus shrugged.

Thomex nodded and swivelled to look at the gate, where the military vehicles were still rolling in.

'Bloody army,' he grunted again.

Nita saw two of the engineers testing the controls on the prototype and went over to interrogate them. Chamus knew how seriously she took his father's test flights and that the two unfortunate men were in for a grilling.

It was peaceful out there in that huge, open airfield. There were no aircraft engines to be heard and a sound he first took to be the wind across his ears now became clearer and he recognised the whispering voices once more.

'Damn the quiet,' his grandfather murmured to himself, 'always got to make yourselves heard in the quiet, haven't you?'

Chamus stared down at him.

'You hear them too?' he blurted out, before he could stop himself.

His grandfather gave him a piercing glare.

'What do you hear, lad?' he asked, as if he already knew the answer.

'I'm not sure,' Chamus said hesitantly. 'It's like a whispering; it's very soft. I thought maybe my eardrums had been damaged. It's like listening to lots of different voices all talking at once, but none loud enough to hear on its own.'

Thomex smiled bitterly and looked away.

'There's nothing wrong with your hearing, Cham. I thought the same when it first started happening to me. But it's got louder over the years and now I know it's not some buzzing in my ears from too many hours behind the engines. I'm not sure what it is, but I think more people hear that sound than want to admit … and I think it *means* something, but I can't work out what. When did you start hearing it, then?'

'After the … the sireniser at the hangar. When my hearing came back.'

His grandfather nodded.

'Mine started after I got shot down. And I didn't damage my ears, I can tell you. I think it has something to do with trauma. It's a curse too, stops you from concentrating, stops you thinking straight. Gets you all tense, too. I can't stand the quiet now. I need noise all the time, and I always have to be doing something, or I get all wound up inside.'

Chamus knelt by his grandfather's wheelchair.

'That's it, that's exactly it,' he agreed excitedly. 'What do you think it is, Grandad? You must have some idea.'

'I don't know, Cham, but it drives me mad. It's like bein' haunted by your own personal ghosts.'

His voice was so harsh when he said it that Chamus stood up again. He looked to where his mother was questioning the two engineers, who were glancing around for some reason to seek shelter.

'I think I will go now, Grandad, if that's okay,' he told the old man, 'I could use a bit of noise.'

His grandfather was in a world of his own. Chamus walked towards his mother and the two men. He waved to her as he drew close and when she turned to him, the men hurried around to the far side of the aeroplane. He told her he was going up and went inside to get his things. When he came out, carrying his kit and wearing his parachute, Nita was talking to the mechanic who had checked his biplane over.

' ... and you've greased all the rocker-box housings?'

'Yes, ma'am. I always do, you know that.'

'And checked the oil?'

'Ma'am ...'

'Sorry, sorry,' she held up her hands. 'You know what I'm like when he's flying, Josek.'

'That I do, ma'am,' the mechanic smiled across at the two engineers by the scout plane. She could have been talking about her son doing a solo in the primitive biplane or her husband doing a test flight in a state-of-the-art, but experimental monoplane. It didn't matter. Nita Aranson did not like either of them taking chances unless she was sure she had done everything she could to make sure they came back down safely.

'Mum, leave him alone,' Chamus sighed. 'He's only been fixing the things for fifteen years.'

She regarded her son carefully.

'Where's your map?' she asked.

'I won't need one,' he protested. 'I'll keep over the main roads once I'm out of the airspace.'

'Young man, you are not flying out of Victovia without a map of the ground you're flying over. Get yourself a map, please.'

'Dad won't have a map.'

'Dad will be happy to get off the ground today. Besides, he's been flying over Bartokhrin all his life. What would he say if he were here now?'

'"Listen to your mother",' Chamus chanted dutifully, painfully aware that the mechanic and the two design engineers were grinning at him.

'Now, inside with you and get whatever maps you need. Where's your scarf? It'll be cold up there.'

'Aw, Mum, will you leave off!'

'Your scarf, young man. And let me see that parachute ...'

He hung his head in embarrassment as his mother checked the straps on his 'chute. Then he went in and grabbed some maps and a scarf and jogged to the plane before she could think of anything else. Climbing into the single-seat cockpit, he strapped himself in and checked the magnetos switch was off. He pressed the small plunger to spray fuel into the carburettor and waved to his mother, who stood by the propeller.

'Be careful up there,' she said. 'Magnetos off?'

'Magnetos off,' he called.

She pulled the propeller through a couple of times and then stood back. He switched the magnetos on.

'Magnetos on,' he called.

With one practised motion she flicked the propeller down and the engine caught with a bellow, the spinning blades blowing her sandy-coloured hair back, and blue smoke billowing from the exhaust. She walked clear and he let the engine warm up for a few minutes. He pulled on his leather flying helmet. His mother wore the same expression that she always wore when she watched him fly, pride mixed with a concern that she tried to hide from him because she knew it bothered him. The canary-yellow biplane had been a gift from his family, a single-seated version of the plane his grandfather had once landed in a pig farm. It was pretty bare by modern standards. The radio was the only concession to modern technology. There was an oil gauge and a fuel gauge and little else in the way of instruments. It had no artificial horizon, no altimeter and was made mainly from doped canvas, wood and aluminium, and the engine was so loud you couldn't hear yourself think. Chamus loved it dearly. It was an animal compared to the tame trainers they flew at school. That was why his grandfather and father insisted he started with it. It never let you forget the basics.

He tabbed the transmit button with his left thumb, requesting clearance. When the tower radioed that he could take his position, he waved to his mother, eased the throttle forward and taxied, rocking and shuddering down to the end of the runway. The windsock halfway along the strip hung limply and the sky was absolutely clear. The controller's voice crackled over his headset, clearing him to take off, and he pushed the throttle open. The engine roared its delight and the plane leapt forward. He felt it go light as it got up to speed, the tailwheel lifted from the ground, he pulled back on the stick and … there was that wonderful, sudden, floating sensation as the wheels left the runway and he was airborne. He peeled away, and the plane that moved like a garden shed on the ground rode the wind with a lazy grace.

Chamus grinned and gunned the engine skywards.

 # Thirteen

Once the excitement had faded and he was left alone with his thoughts, Benyan began to be afraid. He was in the back of a covered truck with six other men; none of whom said anything to him. They passed around cigarettes and played cards and made crude jokes, but he was left to himself at the front, against the wall of the cab.

The voices of the martyrs had died down and were not as clear now, over the growl of the lorry's engine. Without their control, he felt isolated, his stomach tightened uncomfortably and his imagination began to plague him with doubts about what he was supposed to do. Kill Altimans. The very idea of it had seemed so normal when he was training with his friends, charging up hills and practising with their weapons. But now he was on his way to Victovia, a place he had never been, to kill two men and a boy whom he had never met. Altimans. The race who had conquered the skies, who had weapons that could lay a country to waste, and armies that could move like the wind to invade and destroy. And he would be going right into the heart of their empire. The six men would see him to the outskirts of the city, the wall of the plateau, and then he would be handed over to others who would guide him to the home of the Aranson men.

The enormity of it made him tremble. They would kill him; the soldiers and police would find him long before he found his targets and they would kill him. Or perhaps even torture him. He had heard stories from men who had been captured before. Few had ever escaped to tell, but of those who had, some had been tortured in ways they could not have even dreamed, with electricity and chemicals, by doctors who knew how to keep you alive and conscious for a long, long time. Benyan clasped his hands together to stop them shaking and put his head down to pray. The voices became clearer and filled his head. He had only to complete his mission, they promised, and paradise would be his. Their strength filled his body again and he found himself chanting in time with them.

But the knot in his stomach would not go away.

The truck bounced and rumbled along the gravel road for several hours, and then as the sun was reaching up towards noon, they came to a halt. He was beckoned out of the back by the driver, and the six men jumped down with him. They were in a town; he did not recognise it, but they were outside a train station. The clear sky of that morning had become overcast, and a light mist was settling over the street. He was not taken out onto the platform. Instead, he was ushered into a warehouse, where a large wooden crate was lying with its top open.

'The train will take you to the foot of the plateau,' the driver told him, 'but the security there is very tight on the way. The trains are searched by soldiers along the route, and all passengers must pass a checkpoint at the end. They have brought in a new system of identification for work papers and we have not yet managed to forge it successfully. You are to be taken in with a shipment of birds. The crate has a false bottom and there will be boxes of birds placed in over you. It is safe and it will work, but you must be silent and still for several hours.'

Benyan looked in horror at the crate. It was four feet cubed, but the section covered by the false bottom was only two feet deep. He would be barely able to move.

'For Shanna and the cause,' the man said, looking pointedly at him.

'For Shanna and the cause,' he repeated, glaring back.

He climbed over the side into the box and curled up on the floor. The man also gave him a water bottle. Then he gently pushed Benyan down and two others lowered in the false floor. Benyan heard the haunting voices grow louder in his head as the darkness closed down on him. There was some light from the ventilation holes around the sides of the box, but it did not help. He was suddenly terrified. He heard and felt the baskets of live birds being placed in on top of him, and to ease his mind, he pictured all the species he remembered from his home village. There were canaries, doves and budgies, as well as swallows and the herons on the lakes. The shifting and scratching of the birds above him was such that he knew they must be crushed in even more than he was, and that some of them would not survive the trip. His mind came back to the prison he had found himself in. The baskets were pressed down and the pressure in the box changed as the lid was put in place.

The hammering came as a shock, the beats of the hammers jolting through the wood around him and sealing him in as securely as if it had been a coffin. The space was just barely deeper than his shoulders were wide and he would not now be able to straighten his legs or neck until somebody opened the box. He resisted the temptation to push up against the boards above him, knowing that it would only increase the terrible feeling of being trapped. He focused on the faces he had memorised: the two men, one old and crippled, one tall and strong, and the boy who was not much younger than Benyan himself. He wondered what it would feel like to die and he fantasised about paradise, and seeing his parents there. Closing his eyes, he slowed his breathing and prayed to Shanna. The voices swirled in his head, chanting and interfering with his concentration and his prayer, demanding his attention. As if they were separate from her … were they not with her? He felt his hands clench into fists and an overpowering impatience to face his enemies came over him. It would be days still before he got his chance. The voices hissed venomous curses, restless and frustrated.

+ + + +

At the bottom of the loop, the wind cut across the biplane's wings with an airy shriek, Chamus's body going suddenly heavy as he pulled back on the control stick and then levelled the bird out. He pressed down on the rudder bar with his right foot, pulled the stick back and the plane went into a spin. He let it get to the point where he was almost losing it, before spiralling into a dive and pulling up just above the mound of cumulous clouds that appeared under the plane's nose. He frowned. Where had that come from? The day had been completely clear, with nothing more than the odd strand of cloud in the air around him. He had not been paying much attention to the weather, absorbed in hours of playing in the sky, with loops, spins, slow rolls, hammerheads – all the things he couldn't do at school without an instructor sitting in the cockpit with him. Doing a difficult manoeuvre was twice as hard with someone next to you making notes on a clipboard.

But now there was this cloud. He angled the aeroplane around and looked towards the city. He couldn't see it. Everything north-west of him was covered with a thick carpet of cloud, including Victovia. He instinctively looked at his fuel gauge. He had been burning up fuel at a massive rate with all his aerobatics, and now he was running low. He closed the throttle down, adjusted the trim and flew lazily in the direction of the city. Taking out a map, he checked his position. There were few major roads in Bartokhrin that stood out from the air, but he could see a lake and a mountain ridge that appeared on the map. He was miles from the city, but there was a landing strip marked that he might be able to reach, out to his east. He would make for that. Keying the transmit button, he radioed the tower at his home airfield.

'Machel Tower, this is AR71,' he spoke into his mike, 'requesting weather check, over.'

'AR71, Machel Tower, we have complete cloud cover. Heavy fog expected to stay with us until dusk. You have an alternative strip, over?'

'Roger that, Machel Tower,' Chamus replied, 'going to try for Najakis Airfield. I'd appreciate it if you could let my folks know, over.'

'They were asking for you earlier, Chamus,' the controller's voice came back. 'I'll let them know you're alright.'

Chamus turned eastwards and started looking for the small airfield. The band of clouds was creeping with him, and the fog was starting to form along the ground. It was unnerving, seeing the mist just come into being like that. He pushed the throttle forward, in a hurry to close the distance between himself and the airstrip. It should have been visible by now, but everything down there looked the same. He checked his map and heading again. Fog slipped slowly under him and he banked the biplane to keep the grey blur out from beneath his wheels.

He was getting worried now. He might not make the airstrip, or it could already be under the fog. Chamus had never made a forced landing on his own, although he had been with his father on two. Landing in a field was not like landing on a nice flat airstrip; you had to know what to look for. A ditch, a grass bank, even a large animal burrow could flip the aircraft over. He tried to remember what his father had taught him about reading terrain, but he wasn't confident enough of what he saw. Everywhere he looked, the ground seemed to have too many obstacles. He checked his fuel again. He would have to make a decision soon. He could always jump with his parachute, but he could not bear the thought of losing the plane. Gripping the stick, he searched desperately for a place to land. And the longer he hesitated, the more the fog crept across the land.

Chamus watched the needle settle at the bottom of the red on the fuel gauge. He had minutes left. If he wasn't going to land, he should jump immediately, while he could still see a clear piece of ground. That clear piece of ground was getting smaller all the time. He kept flying, hoping for another opportunity. But with a growing sense of dread, he realised he had done what a pilot should never do. He had frozen and lost his chance. Looking back to where the last patch of open space had been, he scowled bitterly. The blanket of fog was now broken only by mountain peaks to his south and east. There was nowhere to go. Even a parachute jump into fog was likely to be fatal.

The engine gave a troubled cough and his heart nearly stopped. This was it. He undid his seatbelt. Better to fall with a parachute than plummet with a plane. He was about to climb out of the cockpit when he saw the space. It was small, but it was there, and one pass over it told him he could get the plane down. He couldn't tell whether he would stop it in time, but beggars could not be choosers. He swung round to bring the plane into the wind and pushed the stick forward.

+ + + +

Rumbler's ears pricked up and he whinnied. Riadni listened hard to the few sounds she could hear in the mist, wondering what the horse's keener hearing had picked up. She had slowed down, careful not to lose her way as the fog settled, and now they were moving at a snail's pace, the girl relying on her horse to watch its footing in the murky haze. There came a noise like a large hornet, growing steadily louder. An aeroplane, but different from the ones she had heard before, rougher and more ragged. She drew Rumbler to a stop to judge its direction as best she could. It was going to pass overhead.

The angry noise bellowed towards them and coughed as it crossed their path. She instinctively soothed Rumbler with some soft words and a pat on the neck, but the old horse was too well trained to rear at the racket created by the machine. Then the hornet coughed again and the racket clattered to a stop, and Riadni knew that the aircraft had not landed and that they did not fly without their engines.

She touched her heels to the horse's flanks and they set off as quickly as they could safely go in the direction that she had last heard the sound. The fog was thinning here and the trail led through a tobacco field lying fallow. Her ears peeled for the sound of a crash, she heard nothing. But that Altiman was definitely out there somewhere.

TWELVE

Chamus could see enough of the ground to get the plane down, but he was going to run into the fog where it crossed the end of the field. Then the engine coughed once, twice and cut out. He cursed at the top of his lungs. He would get only one go at this. He keyed the transmit button on the throttle:

'Mayday, mayday, this is AR71, making a forced landing in low visibility about one hundred and twenty miles south-east of Victovia. Repeat, AR71 making a forced landing in low visibility one hundred and twenty miles south-east of Victovia.'

Then he aimed at the lower edge of the clear area and glided in on the momentum from his dive. The carpet of earth and rough grass came up fast and he pulled back on the stick to lift the nose. The landing gear hit once, bouncing him back up into the air. Then he came down once more, and the main gear touched again. The plane settled back on its tailwheel and then he was bumping along the field, flaps up and brakes on. He was still going too fast and he was careering into the bank of fog ahead of him. There was nothing to do but wait and see if there was more field to go, or if he was going to run into a tree, or the side of a house. But the stretch of flat, rough earth continued and the biplane came to a gradual halt.

He flopped back, undid his seatbelt and parachute straps, and muttered a prayer of thanks as he pulled off his flying helmet and unzipped his jacket. The mist was cool on his skin and he became aware of how much he had been sweating. His whole body was trembling with adrenaline. He felt suddenly exhausted. There were things he should be doing, but he couldn't think. He just wanted to sit back and enjoy being safe for a few minutes.

Eventually, he began to get cold, so he decided he needed to get busy. He tried the radio, but could not get a reception, and reasoned that he must be in a radio shadow. Pulling ropes, a mallet and some metal pins from under his seat, he climbed out of the cockpit. He hammered a pin into the stony ground under the nose, the tail and each of the wingtips and tied the plane down. He might well have to abandon it and he didn't want to leave it at the mercy of any strong winds. Then he pulled out his maps and a compass and tried to gauge his position, but there was still too much fog to spot any landmarks. He took out a wrapped pair of bacon, lettuce and tomato sandwiches that his mother had made him take and ate one while he took stock of his situation.

He was somewhere in Bartokhrin. He was not sure where, but the place was most likely swarming with terrorists, so it was safe to assume that he could well be in danger. He tried the radio again, but there was still no signal. He had almost no food, no water at all and no shelter other than the wing of his plane. Nights in Bartokhrin could get very cold and it was already – he looked at his watch – two o'clock. With the clouds as they were, it could start getting dark by seven. He knew he was supposed to stay by his aircraft and wait for help. Search parties would be setting out already, but Bartokhrin was a massive country, and the position he had given before landing had been rough at best. Chamus wanted to do something; he did not want to wait. If he could find a radio that he could get a signal on, he could call for help, and the search planes could triangulate and find him, or if he could find some fuel, he could try and take off. Whatever he did, he would have to leave the plane un-attended and head out into unknown country. He paced up and down as he considered his options.

Something came whipping out of the mist and wrapped itself around his legs. He lost his balance and fell over, sitting up quickly to see what had knocked him down. It was a belasto, a Bartokhrian hunting weapon. In fright, he strug-gled to untangle it from his legs, but a figure came running at him from behind. He grabbed the mallet that lay by one of the pins and swung at his attacker, who dodged aside and kicked it out of his hand. He lunged at the nimble figure, but his legs were still tied up and he fell again. The Bartokhrian jumped on his back, knocking the wind out of him, and pressed a blade against his throat.

'Don't move,' a voice hissed in his ear.

The Fringelander's other hand pulled his arms up and held them in place with their knees. Chamus felt cord being tied around his wrists and he flinched, but the knife pressed harder against his throat. After his wrists, the belasto was taken from his calves and replaced with another length of cord. In a matter of seconds, he was helpless. The Bartokhrian rolled him onto his back and stood up. Pulling and twisting at his bonds, Chamus gritted his teeth, glared in pure hate at his captor. He wanted to look aggressive, but his mind was back in the hangar, watching the last moments of a suicidal Fringelander.

'Who are you? What do you want?' he asked in a defiant tone.

'You're on my land,' the Bartokhrian replied, and he noted with surprise that it was a girl. 'I'll ask the questions.'

She was dressed in the cotton and rawhide riding clothes of a boy, but had a headscarf and wig, and the strange make-up in keeping with the Shanneyan law that forbade the bare skin of a woman's face to be seen by any man other than her husband. The dark paint around her eyes heightened her hostile glare.

'What are you doing here?' she demanded. 'Are you spying on my family? Are you going to bomb us?'

'I don't know who your family is,' he grunted. 'And I don't care. I'm not even sure where I am, but you have no right to hold me. If anything happens to me, my father will bring the air force down on this place like a ton of bricks.'

It was a hollow threat, but it got a reaction. She stepped back and was silent for a minute. He followed it up.

'All I want is some fuel for my plane and I'll leave. Let me go and get me some fuel, and I'll let you be. I don't want to hurt you, or anything.'

She sneered at him, kicking his bound feet.

'Like that was worrying me. My father told me that your men were more like women, and I thought he was joking. But he was right. Get you out of your machines and you're like shelled snails.'

Chamus tried to rise, but she shoved him down with her foot.

'What's your problem?' he snarled with rage. 'I just want some fuel, some plain old bloody petrol will do. I'll pay you for it. You lot are always happy to take our money, aren't you? Get me some fuel and I'll give you enough to buy yourself a new battleaxe, or something.'

Riadni looked at him contemptuously. She could not help being disappointed with her first encounter with an Altiman. Somehow, she had expected more, not this whining boy who talked down to her, but could not fight his way out of a wet paper bag. But she was fascinated by the aircraft. Turning her back on him, she walked around the plane, touching its varnished canvas fuselage and massive circular engine. She climbed up to peer into the cockpit. There were no signs of any weapons anywhere, but it was hard to tell with their strange science. Seen from the ground, the Altiman flying machines appeared graceful and powerful, but what she saw before her was ugly and strange and looked as if it could fall apart at any moment.

'It's all just held together with wire and wood,' she said to herself.

Chamus craned his neck to follow her movement, anxious that she might damage something.

'That's because it has to be light. It's an old design,' he growled, sensitive about his beloved ragwing. 'It's how planes used to be made. These take more skill to fly.'

Riadni ignored him. She thought the workmanship of the wood and metal was excellent, but the seat looked uncomfortable, the engine stank of oil and smoke and judging by how easily the craft shook under her weight, Rumbler could probably kick the whole thing to pieces if he wanted. She jumped down and gazed at her captive.

'What do you want?' Chamus asked. 'Money? Are you going to hold me hostage? Who are you?'

'My name's Riadni Mocranen. You're on my father's land.'

'I ran out of fuel. I was going to crash. I had to land here. Believe me, I'll be leaving this bloody wasteland as soon as I can get my plane off the ground.'

'You swear a lot.'

'Sod off.'

They glared at each other for a full minute.

'I thought girls weren't allowed to do anything on their own in the Fringelands,' he said suspiciously. 'Why are you alone? There should be other women with you, or a man. Why are you dressed like that? Are you trying to act like a man, is that it? Does anybody even know you're out here?'

'I have you tied up, I have a knife,' Riadni snapped. 'Are you really trying to annoy me? I do what I like, on my own or not. And what do you mean "the Fringelands"?'

'The Fringelands,' he repeated, motioning around him with his head. 'This, all this country around us.'

'This is Kemsemet, in Bartokhrin,' she frowned. 'I've never heard of the Fringelands. What are they on the fringe of?'

'Altima ... I think,' Chamus muttered. He had never thought of it that way.

'Bartokhrin's twice the size of Altima,' Riadni laughed. 'How can *we* be on *your* edge?'

Chamus stayed silent. Actually, Bartokhrin was five times the size of Altima. And it was only one of four Fringeland countries. Now that he thought about it, the name was a bit silly.

'Look,' he said, with the tone of a patient parent dealing with a difficult child, 'you go and get your father, tell him I'll pay him well for some fuel and that I'll leave as soon as the fog clears. And get these ropes off me … now, please.'

Riadni faced him, her hands on her hips. She had heard that women in Altima were allowed do anything the men could, but this boy was the same as all the others she had met. It seemed she could never get any respect. The thought brought Benyan to mind. She wondered how impressed he would be that she had captured an Altiman spy all on her own. She decided to find out. Rumbler was already tired and would not take kindly to another body weighing him down for the rest of the ride to the Hadram Cassal camp. Walking behind Chamus, she grabbed his collar with one hand and a handful of hair with the other and dragged him towards the plane.

'What the hell do you think you're doing?' he shouted fiercely, but there was fear in his voice. 'Get your bloody hands off me!'

She got some satisfaction in knowing he was scared of her, but she was slightly ashamed too. Altiman or not, the boy had done nothing to hurt her. She had attacked him before she even knew anything about him. But then, she knew he was from Altima and he had been flying over their land, and he said his father was in the air force, the same air force that had killed people in Yered and half a dozen other towns. Yanking his brown hair hard enough to make him cry out, she pulled her captive over to the front of the aeroplane. She would leave him wrapped up here, ready for collection. Lakrem Elbeth and Benyan would know what to do with him. They might even get the Altimans to stop their attacks, and then maybe she would get some respect! Sitting him up against the landing gear, she used more cord to tie him securely to the main leg of the gear.

'You want me to go and get someone for you to talk to?' she said primly. 'How about the Hadram Cassal? You know them? Will they do?'

The sudden fear on his face struck doubt into her and for a moment, she wondered if she was doing the right thing. But Elbeth and his men would not hurt an unarmed, helpless boy; they were honourable fighting men. Checking his bonds were secured, she walked back out into the fog to where Rumbler was waiting, his reins wrapped around a fencepost. She undid them and swung up into the saddle. It was still another hour to the Hadram Cassal camp, but the fog was finally burning off around her and it was an easy ride the rest of the way. Riadni cast her eyes back once more at the grey silhouette of the aeroplane in the mist and then set her horse off towards Sleeping Hill.

 ## ELEVEN

eft alone in the enclosed darkness, Benyan lost track of time. It had seemed an age since he had felt the crate being lifted up from the concrete and carried bumping and swaying, to be set down on a different sounding floor; the wooden boards of the train. Then the train had moved off and he could hear the rumble of its engine and the clack-clack of the steel wheels on their tracks. The birds twitched and rustled above him, increasing his sense of isolation. And in the crushing, lonely darkness, the spirits made themselves felt.

All the history his father and uncle had taught him came to life in that tiny, black space. Visions of families burnt alive in their homes for not paying rent to absentee landlords, Shanneyans being branded as criminals and hanged for practising their religion, and of cannon smashing rebel armies armed with swords and knives. There were the markets where men, women and children were bought and sold like cattle for the slave trade and transported to other countries in slave ships, kept in brutal conditions where nearly half of them would die before they reached their destination. With the spirits threading through his consciousness, he relived these events as if he had been there.

At one point, a cramp in his calf brought him back to his own situation and he twisted and contorted to try and stretch the leg out to ease the pain. He managed to quell it slightly by forcing himself into one corner and pushing his foot into the opposite corner, massaging the muscle until the ache died away. In the minutes that followed, he reflected on what he was going to do in Victovia and a part of him wondered about the people he was to kill. Was the death of one person really a reason for causing the deaths of others? And if that were so, where did it stop? People had died throughout history. If someone else had to die for every death caused, how would that make things better for the people who were left? The books of Shanna allowed for revenge, but they also taught forgiveness and respect for others. He closed his eyes to pray for guidance, but as if this opened the door, the spirits came back and plunged him once more into the crimes of the past. And with each vision, he felt a piece of himself being torn away and lost to the pain.

+ + + +

Riadni was careful to observe the camp from a distance before riding in, in case her father, or one of her older brothers, might be there, waiting for her. When she was sure that the coast was clear, she rode up past the herd of cattle and the boy who watched them and approached the caves where she had met Lakrem Elbeth. Suspicious eyes watched her and she knew word had spread long before she reached the foot of the hill. She dismounted near the water trough, loosening the bridle and taking the bit out of Rumbler's mouth. She draped the reins around the railing by the trough, so that he could drink.

Elbeth himself came out to greet her. She swept her eyes around the camp in search of Benyan, but didn't see him.

'Here's our young runaway,' Elbeth said to her as he approached. 'Your father has been looking for you. He is very worried.'

She bowed and then looked straight at him.

'I've left my father's home, Master Elbeth. I want to join the Hadram Cassal and drive the Altimans from our lives.'

He smiled slightly, as if pleased but not surprised.

'This is a hard life that you choose for yourself. Your father would not wish it.'

'My father has made it clear that he does not want me for a daughter,' Riadni replied. 'So if I can't bring him happiness, perhaps I can bring him honour.'

'I think you would be a worthy addition to the cause,' he bowed his head, his eyes giving her a piercing look.

Riadni was surprised that he had accepted her so readily. Tradition did not allow for women to train and fight with men. Nor did he seem surprised with her decision; it was almost as if he had expected her. She cast her gaze around again for Benyan and Elbeth saw the movement.

'Benyan has left us,' he told her, as if reading her thoughts. 'He has moved on to another camp, where he is to complete his training and join our group near the border.'

Riadni could barely contain her disappointment.

'Will he be coming back?' she asked, hating herself for being so obvious.

'No,' Elbeth said solemnly. 'All of our recruits move on from here to other places when they are ready to join the struggle. But I can see a place for a female warrior in his group. The strength of our organisation, Miss Mocranen, is based on family and friendship. We try to keep friends together, for they fight better and are utterly loyal to each other and that is why the Altiman spies fail to infiltrate us. Benyan is your friend, and if you wish, and if you complete your training in time, perhaps we could send you to join him.'

Riadni considered this. She had not expected to go so far from home; the border with Victovia was over a hundred miles away. But then, she reasoned, she had left home and she would not be going back. What did any distance matter?

'Yes,' she nodded, 'I'd like that.'

'Then I will leave you with Master Quelnas,' Elbeth gestured to a hatchet-faced man with thinning hair and two revolvers in holsters on his belt, who was walking towards them. 'He will take you through your initiation and begin your training.'

Riadni recognised him. It was the man who had upstaged Brother Fazekiel at the churchground. He looked at her with amused interest, the kind of expression that men reserved for uppity women. It was always the same.

'Oh!' she exclaimed. 'I almost forgot! Master Elbeth, I caught an Altiman. A pilot, just a boy, really. He's tied up back at his aeroplane. He had to land when he ran out of fuel and I captured him.'

Elbeth turned towards her and for a moment the friendliness in his eyes was gone, replaced only by a hungry, empty stare. Then he beamed and clapped his hands.

'Off to a flying start, young Riadni!' he laughed. 'Where is this boy-Altiman? We must secure him at once. Quelnas, did you hear that? The girl has barely joined the order and already she has claimed her first kill!'

Riadni's heart froze. They were going to kill the boy. That should not have shocked her, but it did. Everyone knew that this was what the Hadram Cassal did, they did away with Altimans. The idea of killing brutal oppressors was something she could approve of; it was the only language the Altimans could understand. But killing a boy her age, who had made the mistake of landing in the wrong field and who was tied up and helpless, was the act of a coward. She decided that she had misread Elbeth's intentions. He had just used the word 'kill' in the same way that men always used it in conversation – to be aggressive and threatening, not meaning it in its real sense. Just as she had threatened the Altiman with her knife, she would not have killed him. She simply needed him to keep still while she tied him up.

'Mount up, Riadni!' Elbeth waved to her. 'Take Quelnas to where you've stashed this young pilot. I look forward to meeting him.'

Quelnas was calling to four other men, and horses were being saddled. She walked back over to Rumbler and took her time readjusting his bridle. Doubt clouded her thoughts and she wanted time to think this through. But the men were already up on their mounts and waiting for her. Quelnas raised his eyebrows in a questioning look and she detected a hint of scorn in his expression. She stuck her foot in the stirrup and lifted herself onto Rumbler's back, avoiding the hard gaze of the fighter. She tapped her heels to Rumbler's flanks and set him off at a canter, getting ahead of the group of men.

Quelnas caught up and rode beside her.

'So where exactly is this pilot?' he asked, in the tolerant tone that men reserved for discussing the trivial matters of women.

'I can't tell you exactly,' she replied. 'The fog was even heavier then. I know the way back. It's about an hour out to the north-west.'

'And you're quite sure this boy you caught was an Altiman?' one of the other, younger men asked from behind her.

Riadni couldn't see his face, but she could tell from his voice that he was smiling. She ground her teeth. Even when she did everything possible to prove herself equal to men, they laughed at her; it wasn't fair.

'There's always the chance that he was just some poor cowherd boy that I beat up for not showing me respect,' she retorted, 'but then that would mean that he's tied to some-one else's aeroplane.'

Some of the men chuckled and she knew she had scored a point. They rode on along the trail as it wound past fields of dry earth, struggling crops and yellowing grass. They had been on the road for about twenty minutes, when Elbeth's words began to trouble her again. She was sure that they would not kill a defenceless boy, but would they even tell her if that was what they intended to do? They would proba-bly think her too innocent yet, to involve in any bloodshed. She looked towards Quelnas, who had not said a word since first asking about the boy.

'What will you do when you have him?' she asked. 'Will you kill him immediately, or will you need to question him first, to see what he's doing here?'

He turned his narrow face towards her and his expression was unreadable.

'We'll do whatever Master Elbeth wants us to do with him,' he answered.

'And what do you think that will be? What do you normally do?'

'Whatever is best for the cause,' Quelnas faced the road again.

'We'll ask him a few questions and then send him home,' another voice piped up.

'Well, the *important* bits of him anyway,' a third added and the others laughed.

Quelnas glanced round at them and the laughing stopped abruptly. He threw a quick look at Riadni and she knew he was checking her reaction. It told her all she needed to know. She caught her breath. They were going to do it. Was this what it meant to be in the Hadram Cassal? She remembered what her father had said about them – that they did the horrible things that normal people could not. But she had taken that to mean killing the well-armed Altiman soldiers and the businessmen they protected, not torturing and murdering a helpless boy in the name of Bartokhrian freedom. And now she was helping them do it. The horses trotted onwards and Riadni knew she had to make a firm decision whether or not she was willing to do this, otherwise she had to do something to lead them away. Every minute that passed took them nearer to the aeroplane. They were already close enough to find it on their own with a bit of searching. She had to do something soon, or be a part of the young pilot's death. She shook her head. What had she been thinking?

At the next fork in the trail, she turned right instead of left, careful to look certain about where she was going. Quelnas stopped, looking down the left-hand fork.

'You said north-west,' he called. 'That path goes north.'

'It's down this way,' she called. 'That turns west further down. This path bears to the left.'

She kept her face turned away as she said it, not wanting to face his harsh stare. After a few seconds, she heard the other horses follow her. Lifting her head, she surveyed the terrain ahead of her. The path would bear right and not left as she'd said, and not long after they would realise she was misleading them. She needed to break away from them, and soon. Their horses were fresh and in better shape than Rumbler. She could not outrun them. But she knew the terrain and the thinning fog would help too. When she came to where the track started to climb gently, she knew this would be her only chance. Goading Rumbler into a gallop, she took off at breakneck speed up the trail. Quelnas shouted after her and she heard all the horses break into a sprint behind her. She would need to time this just right.

The track crested the hill not far ahead and she drove Rumbler frantically for the top. He was already tired from the day's ride and did not have much steam left, but she had to get far enough ahead to disappear from sight over the crest. At the top there was a copse of trees to her right and a high bank to her left and she hauled back on the reins just as she passed it, bringing Rumbler almost to a halt and pulling him hard to the right just in time to make a hairpin turn that cornered over a steep, scree-covered slope. It was hidden from sight of the others and she waited behind the trees as the men careered over the crest in the track and failed to slow down in time to make the bend.

Quelnas was the first, and when he saw the edge, he did not attempt the turn, slowing his horse down as best he could and letting it jump off the edge and scramble straight down the loosely covered slope into the fog that hid the bottom. The two that followed him saw him disappear and tried to make the turn in the track, but their horses were going too fast. One slid onto its side, pinning its owner under it; the other skidded over the edge and threw its rider. It used its momentum to pick itself up and clambered down after the man who tumbled ahead of it. The remaining two were right behind their comrades and galloping at full tilt. With the high bank on one side and the fallen horse blocking their path on the other, there was nowhere for them to go but over the edge. Leaning right back as the horses dropped over the lip of the edge, they managed to stay in their saddles, but their momentum carried them scrambling to the bottom. The fallen horse got up from the road and nuzzled its fallen rider, who groaned, but made no attempt to get up.

Riadni watched, her heart in her throat with excitement. She spared the men on the slope a quick look, knowing they would not be able to stop until they reached the wide stream at the bottom and that there was no way up for the horses for a couple of miles in either direction. She felt a bit sorry for the horses, but not the men. Giving a nervous giggle, she patted Rumbler's neck.

'Attaboy, you showed 'em. Who's the best horse, eh? You are. Yes you are!'

Rumbler was panting hard, but she eased him into a trot and headed back down the way she had come. They would find their way out eventually and when they did, they would come looking for her … and for the pilot. Even as she rode down the hill, the seriousness of what she had done settled in on her. She had betrayed the Hadram Cassal. Pushing the newly awakened fear to the back of her mind, she set off towards the aeroplane and its grounded pilot.

+ + + +

Chamus tried hard to ignore the whispering that wheedled its way into his thoughts. His teeth clenched as he tensed against the cords that bound him. The knots were good. No matter what he tried, he could not loosen them. The sun was high in the sky. He guessed it was after four o'clock. The fog was lifting and the wing over his right shoulder no longer offered any shade. The sun's diffused glow kept his eyes levelled at the ground most of the time. He was uncomfortable, hungry and very thirsty. His feelings swung from fear of the terrorists he knew were on their way, to rage at the girl who had attacked him, to shame that he had been beaten in a fight by a girl without even getting in any decent hits. Just as well for her, he thought. All in all, the day had not turned out well and he fully expected it to get worse. And he could really do without those aggravating bloody *voices*. The frustration boiled over and he let it out with a roar. It was sucked up by the diminishing fog, so he let rip with another one. It felt good to get it out of his system.

But the silence won back the air. He was surprised that there were few sounds of nature – no grasshoppers or birds – and he wondered if it was an effect of the fog. Just as he was about to let out another bellow, he heard the beat of hooves and fear set his heart racing. A horse and rider materialised out of the mist and he recognised the girl. What was her name again? Riadni. She seemed to be on her own. There was no one with her. No Hadram Cassal. He scowled. He'd been had. She probably just went home for lunch to let him stew in his own imagination. Chamus swore viciously, but then calmed himself down. She would let him loose now; her game was over. But if she thought he was angry, she might take off again and leave him.

Riadni swung down off her horse and strode over to him.

'We don't have a lot of time,' she said. 'So just shut up and listen. The Hadram Cassal are on their way …'

'Oh, right,' he said, nodding, the disdain evident on his face. 'Good mates of yours, are they?'

This was not the reaction Riadni had expected. He didn't believe her and that meant she was going to have to spend precious time arguing with him.

'Do you want to be untied, or wait and see if I'm joking?' she asked, eyebrows raised and fists on hips. 'I can leave right now. You can't.'

He was about to say something else, but stopped.

'I was going to hand you in,' she continued. 'I told them you're here, but I found out they were going to kill you …'

'Fancy that ...'

' ... and I'm not about to give them a hand to murder a helpless boy. So, I'm going to let you loose and then get out of here. I suggest you don't make a big thing of this, forget getting even with me, or anything like that. Just go, okay?'

She could see the muscles of his jaw tense up, contempt written all over his face, but then he relaxed and nodded. Putting her knife back in its scabbard, she crouched down by him and untied his bonds. He rubbed his wrists and ankles to get the circulation back into them and then stood up stiffly. Honour demanded that he now flatten her in true schoolyard fashion, but there were three problems: a) she was a girl, b) she was pretty tough for a girl, in fact she was pretty tough for a boy, and c) there was a chance that she wasn't lying about the Hadram Cassal.

She caught the look on his face. Walking away from him, she jumped up into the saddle.

'I lost them back out to the east, but they'll find you soon enough,' she warned. 'You should get going. They'll be looking for you, and they're going to be after me too now. So don't waste time starting anything, alright? Just go.'

'What do you mean, just go?' he demanded. 'You're going to take off on your horse and leave me here, after telling them where I am? You can make room up there for me. I'm coming with you.'

He ran to the cockpit and grabbed his things.

'What?' Riadni's mouth dropped open.

'They're on horses, right? So what chance have I got of outrunning them? Let me up. I'm coming with you!'

'Rumbler doesn't let strangers ride him.'

'Oh ... sorry. I didn't know the horse was in charge. Should I be talking to him?'

'Look, he's old and we've been riding all day. He can't take the extra weight,' Riadni protested, but she could see the desperation on the boy's face. 'Men don't ride with women! It's forbidden!'

'If they catch me, I'm dead,' Chamus pleaded. 'I know what they're like. I've seen them do it before. I can't outrun a horse and I have nowhere to go. Please. Let me go with you.'

She looked away. Rumbler was going to be slow enough as it was. He was worn out and thirsty and he was too old to be carrying two riders.

'Alright,' she sighed. 'Get on.'

Taking her foot out of the stirrup, she turned it out for him and held Rumbler still, so that Chamus could climb up, but he found it more difficult than it looked. He had been on pony treks twice before, but had never done any real riding, and having somebody already in the saddle didn't help. He grabbed the pommel with his left hand, put his left foot in the stirrup and went to heave himself on, but the stirrup turned and his swinging leg missed the back of the horse. He fell back and dropped his foot to the ground again, but the other one stayed caught in the stirrup and he nearly lost his balance. He tried again, managing to get his foot onto the back of the saddle, but lunged so hard doing it that Rumbler stepped sideways and Chamus was forced to drop back again.

'Stop, *stop*,' Riadni held up her hand. 'Give me your bag, okay? Right, now, on the count of three, you swing up. One ... two ... three ...'

He managed to get his right foot onto the back of the saddle. Riadni grabbed his right sleeve and dragged him up behind her, giggling despite herself. Chamus found that the saddle was too small for both of them and he was now sitting on the hard cantle at the back. He bore the discomfort and said nothing. She took the stirrup back off him.

'Keep your hands off,' she warned solemnly. 'I know about you Altimans.'

Rumbler whinnied in protest at the extra weight, but set off at a brisk walk at her touch. Riadni knew he was on his last legs, but they had to reach a well-travelled road and lose their tracks as soon as they could. She didn't know where to go. She could not go home. They would look for her there, and her betrayal would cause enough problems for her family as it was. Rumbler needed rest, grass and water and they would need shelter for the night. The boy behind her was uncomfortably close, and did not know how to ride a horse. She wanted to be rid of him as soon as possible. Turning south, she aimed for the jagged hills, dropping down into a shallow stream to keep below the horizon and help hide their tracks. Rumbler battled wearily forward with his new burden as his mistress tried to work out how to stay ahead of the Hadram Cassal.

 **T**ɛп

Benyan felt as if a horde of ghosts had passed through his head, but these new ones were different. He could make out individuals; there were personalities who were making themselves felt, eager to share their grief with him. The more time that passed, the less control he had over his body and mind, and he mourned the loss. He closed his eyes wearily and succumbed once more to the force of the spirits' memories.

He was a group of three men and two women, brothers and sisters of the Lentton family, his soul sharing five bodies at once. He did not question how it was possible. There was no need; it simply was. They lived in the town of Exurieth, which lay in the shadow of the plateau city of Mauraine. It was a Bartokhrian town in Altiman territory and it had been the scene of protests for years. The waste from factories in Mauraine was contaminating the farmland around Exurieth, poisoning its crops, killing livestock and spreading sickness through the town's water supply. In court, the lawyers acting for the factory owners had proved, in theory, that this could not be true. But the crops and the animals still died.

The Lenttons responded by going out one night and filling some of the pipes that spilled the waste with bags of cement. Benyan enjoyed taking part in the sabotage, dressed in fisherman's waders, waterproofs and heavy gloves to protect his skin from the toxic slurry. They worked quickly to stack up the heavy paper bags of cement while the flow had slacked off. The flow would start again slowly enough to soak into the cement and create a serious blockage. When he was done, he congratulated each other and slapped each other on the backs. They were proud of himself. His town was not going to let themselves be pushed around by the faceless men in suits. The contaminated waste in the blocked pipes backed up and four factories in Mauraine had to be evacuated the following day because of the poisonous fumes that filled the buildings.

A few nights later, the five of him got together again and set out to block the remaining pipes that were contaminating their land. One of him kept watch while the others unloaded the bags of cement. The fumes in the first pipe they came to were different from the others; they smelled of petrol and other chemicals. His torches waved around the dark opening in the wall of a ditch, taking in the slow trickle of the chemical slurry from the gaping mouth of the corrugated pipe. All five of him covered their mouths with wet neckerchiefs to help against the fumes as they stacked the heavy sacks.

They were halfway through when a bright spotlight suddenly lit the area. He was surrounded. Men armed with guns stood on the walls of the ditch, hidden in the shadows behind the lights. He shielded his faces from the glare, trying to identify the silhouettes who shouted down to them. They ordered all of him to finish blocking the pipe. Frightened and confused, he did as they were told, shoving handfuls of loose cement into the gaps that remained between the bags. The five Lenttons turned to face the men behind the light, wanting to get out of that ditch and get back to his homes. Then someone lit a flare and he realised with sudden terror that they were standing knee-deep in a pool of the petro-chemical slurry. The flare was tossed into the ditch and Benyan died five burning deaths.

He was screaming when the top of the box opened and three pairs of strong hands pulled him up into a light that scorched his eyes.

'Turn off some of the lights,' a voice said. 'By Shanna, this one's far gone.'

He fell to the floor and thrashed around, still suffering from the flames that had disappeared with the vision. Soon, he was able to feel the cool floor and his eyes adjusted to the dim light. But Benyan Akhna no longer looked out from those eyes. Between him and his senses, the Lenttons had taken up residence. Five vengeful spirits looked up from the floor of the dark freight depot, hungry for others to share their fate. The last and strongest images from Benyan's consciousness came to the fore, a picture of two men and a fourteen-year-old boy.

+ + + +

Evening was falling and Chamus and Riadni walked the last two miles to take the strain off Rumbler, who was close to collapse. Chamus shouldered the heavy saddlebags, while

Riadni carried his knapsack and parachute rig, leading the horse by its reins. The trail she had chosen led into the foothills of the heavily forested Enkantra Mountains, towards a well concealed spring where they could rest. The fog had lifted and the day was fresh and clear as it approached twilight. They both kept looking back to search the hillside and landscape beneath them for signs of their pursuers, but they could see nothing.

'We can stop here,' Riadni said finally, leading Rumbler to the stream that ran from the base of a small waterfall, where he greedily lapped up gulps of the fresh water.

Chamus dropped the saddlebags immediately and rolled his tired shoulders. He swivelled slowly to take in their surroundings. They were in an oblong clearing encircled by trees, with the spring at one end, sending a stream flowing along its length and down the slope at the other. Walking to the downhill end, he could see for miles. There were signs of movement at several points in the distance, but nothing appeared to be coming their way.

'How many of them are there?' he asked.

'Sorry?'

'The Hadram Cassal, how many of them are there?'

Riadni sat on the bank downstream from where the horse was drinking, and pulled off her boots and socks, sinking her bare feet into the soothing water.

'There's maybe forty or fifty at the camp. But they're all over the country, even in Altima and other places. Altogether there's hundreds, maybe even thousands of them.'

'How many do you think will come after us?'

Riadni shrugged, kicking her feet gently back and forth.

†ЕП

How did he expect her to know? She wondered how long he intended to stay around, hoping he would just take some water and go his own way. She had some food, but not a lot, and she was dying to take off her wig, her head was itching with the heat and sweat. He sat down nearby and sprawled out on the grass.

'Where are you going to go from here?' she asked.

'I don't even know where "here" is,' he replied. 'Where are we?'

'The northern end of the Enkantra range,' she told him. 'Mount Harna.'

'That means nothing to me whatsoever,' he grunted, holding his hand up to shield his eyes from the sun shining over the edge of the treeline.

Riadni sighed quietly. He didn't seem to be going anywhere soon. Chamus got up and rooted around in his knapsack. He took out his maps, and the second of the sandwiches his mother had made him. He tore the sandwich in two.

'Want some?' he asked her.

Riadni hesitated.

'What's in it?' she asked.

'Bacon, lettuce and tomato,' he said. 'It won't kill you.'

'Thanks.' It was rude to refuse a gift of food, so she took it and nibbled on it, feeling embarrassed that she had not offered any of her own supplies. Opening one of the saddlebags, she took out a small loaf of bread, some hummus and some apples. She held the food up. 'Help yourself.'

They ate in silence, washing the simple meal down with water. Riadni filled her water canteens in the plunge pool of

129

the waterfall and noticed that Chamus did not do the same.

'Don't you have a water bottle?' she asked.

'I was up for a few hours' flight,' he said, pulling his shoes off and walking up to the pool. 'I didn't come equipped for a mountain trek.'

'Not in the pool!' she snapped, causing him to jump. 'Don't you know anything? Wash downstream from where you drink.'

He was about to retort, but thought the better of it, walking around her and dipping his feet in lower down the stream instead.

'I'm going into the hills,' she told him. 'I'll have to wait a few days before I can go home. I'm not even sure if I can go home. Altima is a long way away. If I were you, I'd get going as soon as I could.'

Chamus opened a map and turned it on his lap to orientate it with his compass. He did not seem to be listening, intent on finding some of the landmarks they had passed, but she was sure that he had heard her. He took a measurement from the base of the map and used his finger and thumb to gauge a distance.

'The edge of Victovia is about a hundred and twenty-five miles away,' he said. 'I don't know how long it will take to walk that far, but I'm guessing maybe a week, probably more. That's assuming I don't get lost, kidnapped or killed along the way. What do you think my chances are without a guide?'

Riadni's eyes narrowed.

'What are you getting at?'

'What I'm getting at is that you know your way around,

but you have nowhere to go. I have somewhere to go, but no way of getting there. I'll pay you to guide me home.'

Riadni was going to scoff at the idea, but then changed her mind. It was true, she had nowhere to go. She had damned herself when she had led those men over the edge of the hill. If she went home, Elbeth and his men would find her there. She could try hiding with other relatives; they had enough of them, but the danger was the same wherever she went. Except Altima. She could be safe there, and the further away she was, the safer her family would be.

'How much would you pay me?' she asked, suspiciously.

He smiled, laying the map to one side.

'My family would be pretty rich by your standards. They'll be very happy to see me safe. How much would you want?'

Riadni bit her lip. This could really work out.

'Thirty crowns,' she stuck her chin out. It was the highest number she dared think of, maybe too high. It would buy a healthy pony. But her mother had taught her to haggle for everything at the market.

Chamus frowned, pretending to think about it. Thirty crowns was about the price of a decent overcoat. He looked up at the sky, really milking the moment, keeping one eye on the expression on her face, which was, to her credit, completely deadpan.

'No, I couldn't,' he said at last, watching her face drop a fraction. 'Make it fifty crowns and we have a deal.'

For a moment she thought he had no idea how to haggle. Then what he was saying sank in and she cursed quietly to herself. She could have gone much higher. Still, fifty crowns was fifty crowns.

'There goes my plane. I probably won't see her again,' he muttered and she heard a note of sorrow in his voice.

'How can you miss a machine?' she asked.

'It's not just a *machine*,' he said, too quickly, and then tried to explain, 'it's an aeroplane, *my* aeroplane. When I'm not flying it's, well, it's …'

He hesitated, seeing the patient tolerance on her face.

'It's like being a fish, anchored to the bottom of a pond,' he said, finally. 'Do you know what I mean?'

'Sort of.'

'That'll have to do. I can't think of a better way to describe it.'

Faced with spending the next week with a strange boy, Riadni began to think of all the complications that that would involve. He seemed to know very little of how to behave with girls – women – and it would be very awkward telling him. Also, they had no shelter, when they should have had a tent each. The events of the day suddenly took their toll on her and she felt tense and exhausted. Chamus was absorbed in his map, and she did not want to talk to him anyway; he was already being much too familiar.

Taking her grooming tools from a saddlebag, she brought them over to Rumbler and after taking off his saddle, blanket and bridle, started brushing the dust and oily, dried sweat from his coat. The grooming relaxed her as much as it did the horse and she took her time, stroking the stiff brush down his back, flanks and legs. When that was done, she went to work with the softer body brush and then cleaned around his hooves with a pick. She felt better, more normal, afterwards and wrapped her arms around the horse's neck, holding her face against him for a while. What machine could ever compare to a horse?

Chamus leaned back on his elbows and looked at the land that was visible between the trees in the failing light. A hundred and twenty-five miles. They might find help before that, but he had to prepare for the worst. A hundred and twenty-five miles across unknown territory, with only an aging horse and a girl no older than himself guiding him and a gang of insane terrorists hunting them all the way. He shook his head and put the map away. Next time he'd keep a closer eye on the weather.

 **Пiпе**

Riadni woke suddenly and was taken aback by the glowing white material that hung over her. It took a few moments to remember the events of the day before and then she recalled how the boy, Chamus, had pulled this massive, round sheet from his pack and made a tent out of it by hanging it from the branch of a tree. It was made of silk and must have been worth a lot of money. He had said it was for people who jumped out of aeroplanes. She had taken that to mean it was a burial shroud, but he assured her it was for slowing a person's fall, not for wrapping them up afterwards.

She ran the back of her hand down the light, slinky folds, admiring the feel of it. Outside, she could hear Chamus moving around. She found herself wondering where Benyan was, and what it would be like to be on the run with him, instead of this irritating Altiman. Riadni smiled to herself. That would be worth getting in trouble for.

She and Chamus had taken turns to keep watch during the night, wishing they could light a fire, but not daring to in case it attracted attention. Taking a small mirror from her bag, she took some time to paint her face. Then, she put on her wig, ducked under the edge of the parachute and looked out. He was reading a small booklet. She wondered if it was a scripture for the false god that the Altimans worshipped. She stood up and stretched, then strolled over to where the boy was sitting and bent over to look at the front cover. It read, 'Guidelines for a Survival Situation'.

'What's a survival situation?' she asked.

'This is,' said Chamus, holding out his hands. 'What we're in now. This is a survival situation.'

She looked around, trying to see what there was to survive. Failing to see any imminent danger, she shrugged and walked over to the tree near the stream, where Rumbler was tied. She held the sides of his head and kissed him on the nose.

'Morning, beautiful,' she whispered. 'How's my hero, you feeling better?'

Chamus looked at her quizzically, then turned back to his reading.

'If you two would like some time alone, I'll wait in the tent,' he quipped. 'Otherwise, I think we need to get going.'

Riadni made a rude gesture behind his back, but then went to saddle the horse. Chamus pulled down the makeshift tent and carefully folded the parachute back into its pack. Opening out a map, he called Riadni over.

'What route do you think we should take?'

She studied the sheet of lines and symbols. There were names and numbers written all over it, with rivers marked in blue and roads in solid black. It was nothing like the hand-drawn maps she had seen before. There were things on it that she did not understand, but it looked scientific and exact. It must be easier to make maps, she thought to herself, when you can look down at the land from above. She found the main road out of Kemsemet, and followed it north-west with her finger to the town of Naranthium.

'We need to go this way, but they will have put the word out and there will be people looking for us. We can cut through the fields a lot, and stay in the hills as much as possible, but there are going to be times when we'll have to take the road. It will take us all of today and part of tomorrow to get to here, Naranthium, but I have cousins there who will hide us for the night and give us food.'

They packed up the last of their things and Chamus watched as Riadni covered up the signs of their stay as best she could. He could not help but be impressed by her. She was smart and capable, even if she was a bit of a tomboy. He thought about the girls in his class, a few of whom he fancied. They were clever and educated and knew they were starting to get sexy, and he wondered how Riadni acted when she was with other girls. Probably giggled and chattered with the best of them, he thought. He looked up at her as she waited impatiently for him to get up on the horse. No, he thought again, probably not. He climbed into the saddle with slightly more dignity than the day before, but not much more, and shifted around as he tried to get his backside comfortable on the hard edge of the cantle.

'When we get to where people might see us, you'll have to get off,' she said, tightly. 'A boy riding in the same saddle as a girl would attract a lot of attention. And it could get you put in the stocks.'

'That's where they throw rotten vegetables at you, right?' he asked.

'No,' she replied, 'for touching a girl who is not your wife, they throw stones. Big ones.'

'Right. Well, let me know when it's time to walk then.'

They rode in silence for a while, Chamus's backside bouncing against the saddle as Rumbler made his way downhill. It was wearing on Riadni's nerves and she fantasised again of being on the run with Benyan, the two of them braving the world together. Rumbler trotted down a steep incline and Chamus was tipped forwards suddenly, his weight falling against Riadni. She gritted her teeth and elbowed him back.

'For the love of Shanna, will you get off me! And stop bouncing around. You're riding like a block of wood!'

'It's not my fault!' he protested. 'I can't help it if I never learned to ride. I didn't have to. We have cars where I come from ...'

'Don't you start with me again!'

'Alright, alright. Look, I'm having to learn this as I go. Give me a chance, okay?'

Riadni closed her eyes for a moment and willed herself to calm down.

'Try and move with him,' she told him. 'Grip with your knees and follow his rhythm. That way it's more comfortable for both of you – and me.'

'I'm trying,' he said. 'It's not easy.'

Then, wanting to change the subject, he asked, 'So, how well do you know the terrorists then?'

'What terrorists?'

'The Hadram Cassal. The murdering scum we're running from. *Those* terrorists.'

Riadni's lip curled.

'They're freedom fighters,' she snapped.

'They're terrorising us,' he put in. 'That is why we're running across the country on a horse, isn't it? Because they're going to kill us both?'

'I betrayed them ... and you're the enemy.'

'Oh, well that's alright then. As long as they have a good reason. Bunch of murdering cowards if you ask me. I suppose the innocent people they kill are fair game, yeah? Our soldiers have to act like soldiers, but it's alright for your lot to sneak into our cities and murder people, right?'

Incensed once more, she stopped the horse and turned to look in his face.

'Innocent? Since when did you care about that? You've been killing our people for centuries, but when we do it back to you, we're animals. What, are you blind? Don't you even know what happens out here? And as for "sneaking" into your cities, what else can we do? Get together in an army, out in the open, so we can get slaughtered by your machines? The Hadram Cassal are fighting the only way they can. And you think they're cowards? Tell me, what takes more courage, to walk into the heart of your enemy's country, knowing you're going to die, or to drop bombs on people's heads from thousands of feet in the air?'

Chamus was struck by the ferocity of her expression and realised that she was not the friend he thought she was. She was still a Fringelander after all. What hope was there of explaining the difference to her? They were all fanatics.

'And stop jolting the saddle!' she added. 'Move with the horse, or you're walking from here on.'

'For God's sake! I'm trying, alright?'

The two said very little to each other after that.

Two hours' ride brought them to the outskirts of a small village called Veron. Chamus got down and walked alongside the horse. Riadni knew people from this village, but she was worried that there were a lot of Hadram Cassal supporters here. Veron was set back in the hills and had few visitors. Not many people were attracted to an area laid waste by strip mining. They didn't like outsiders and Altima was about as outside as you could get. It was Altiman businessmen who had come, promising to make the villagers rich and had left, taking their money with them and leaving nothing but a ravaged landscape and the livelihood of the village's trappers and gold prospectors in ruins, along with the storekeepers who depended on their trade. Chamus listened to the story of Veron and wished he looked more like a Bartokhrian. Walking along a trail that bypassed the village, he was painfully conscious of his city-style clothes and pale skin. He stuck out like a sore thumb.

'I need to change my clothes,' he muttered to Riadni.

'Yeah,' she grunted, 'that way you can look like an Altiman disguising himself as a local. You're as pale as a plucked chicken and you have yellow hair. It's going to take more than a change of clothes to hide who you are.'

The track took them along the edge of some woods, avoiding the main streets in the village. People peered from their windows at them, and some even came out to stare. Riadni felt embarrassed, both for being with this Altiman, but also for him. She knew that no matter how self-conscious she was feeling, it must be ten times worse for him.

Suddenly, a horseman appeared out of the trees and blocked their path. He was dressed in trapper's clothes of fur and skin, his face was burnt a deep brown and he was missing most of his teeth. He held a belasto in one hand and a machete in the other. Riadni went to turn Rumbler around, but then saw what Chamus had already seen, another man on foot behind them, similarly armed.

'Stand away, girl,' the first one said. 'That boy's worth money to us.'

'Get on,' Riadni hissed quietly.

Chamus glanced back at the man in front of them and knew he was only going to get one chance at this. And he just wasn't that good at getting on a horse. He bolted for a low stone wall instead and Riadni kicked Rumbler into action, racing ahead. Chamus leapt onto the wall, ran along it and jumped from the end onto the horse's back as Riadni slowed to catch him. A belasto caught him around the ankle as his foot left the wall, but missed his other leg. Riadni steered Rumbler down into the village along a laneway walled in by ramshackle adobe buildings on either side. Chamus shook the weapon loose from his leg and let it drop to the ground.

'Keep your head low!' she called, as they charged down the narrow lane. 'Don't let them get the belastoes round your neck!'

They burst out the other end into the main street and as Riadni leaned to take a hard left, Chamus had to resist the urge to lean the other way and right himself. Galloping on a horse was hard work and his backside was taking a batter-ing. He risked a glance behind them and saw that the mounted trapper was close behind, swinging another belasto. He could not see the second man. But then ahead of them, somebody on horseback swept in from their left; the man had a horse after all.

'Come on, boy!' Riadni shouted and ran Rumbler right at the other horse.

The horse shied away from the charge and the man was nearly thrown, but held on. Rumbler galloped past and on down the street. The two trappers were right on their heels. Riadni urged her steed on even faster, and then broke right and down another lane, turning so fast that Chamus almost fell off. The lane dropped down a steep hill and there were wooden-walled clay steps near the bottom that caused Rumbler to slow suddenly, his long strides pulled short by the narrow footing. The end of the lane was half blocked by a large barrow and Rumbler leapt straight over it.

This time Chamus did fall, tumbling back out of the saddle and landing in the front of the barrow, thrusting the handles upwards. He cried out as his ribs and hip hit the wood, then curled into a ball as the first horseman jumped over him. But the handles caught one of the horse's forelegs and it landed badly, throwing its rider. The second was coming down the steps slower and reined in his horse in time to stop before the upturned barrow. Chamus got to his feet, jumped out of the barrow and delivered a sound kick at the fallen trapper's head, before grabbing his belasto and machete and running to catch up with Riadni. The second rider pushed the barrow out of the way with his foot and charged after them. They were in a lane that ran down the backs of the buildings, and Chamus darted into a narrow gateway as he saw the trapper swing his belasto again. The weapon slapped off the wall where Chamus had been an instant earlier. He popped his head around again in time to see Riadni's belasto wrap itself around the man's neck. He was caught off-guard, but stayed on his horse. Her belasto only had wooden weights and he managed to quickly loosen it enough to breathe.

But it gave Chamus enough time to get back on behind Riadni and they raced up to the other end of the village again. Rumbler's hooves drummed a track up along a laneway strewn with clotheslines, where Riadni knew the belastoes would be harder to use. Thinking of the pistol in her bag, she cursed herself for not having it ready. Glancing back, she saw both trappers coming after them again. Ducking under one row after another of hanging clothes, Chamus clung to Riadni's waist as she urged her horse onwards. The first trapper was almost on top of them, when Chamus swung the machete out and cut one of the lines, dropping it right onto the man behind them. The trapper was forced to slow to rid himself of the entanglement.

They came out the other end of the lane, back onto the main street, and there were others out now to watch the chase. Riadni spared a glance around to see if anyone else was going to try and get in their way, but for the moment it seemed to be just the two hunters. The rest just watched, keen to see an Altiman get what was coming to him, or simply unwilling to interfere. She turned Rumbler to the right and headed for the road that led up into the stand of tall pines ahead, weaving him from one side to the other to avoid the belastoes. A man in an apron ran out from a store and made as if to grab them, but Chamus swung the machete, cutting a gash in the man's forearm.

Rumbler whinnied with excitement and adrenaline, and Riadni shouted encouragement to him, relishing the chase. He was twice the age of the horses behind him, but was better fed and trained and even with the two teenagers and loaded saddlebags, he was outrunning their pursuers. Riadni looked back and saw the trappers falling behind. But they were not giving up and she knew that they could simply track Rumbler and bide their time if they lost sight of their quarry. When they were far enough into the trees, she slowed Rumbler to a fast trot to conserve his energy. She didn't know what to do. Those men would be skilled trackers, and they would know that she and Chamus would have to stop somewhere.

Behind her, she heard Chamus grunt in pain and remembered his fall.

'Are you alright?' she asked.

'I'll live,' he wheezed. 'Just bruises, I think. But my bum's killing me. How are we going to lose these two? They're not Hadram Cassal, are they?'

'No, I don't think so. Probably just thought they could hold you for ransom.'

She thought about the land ahead of them.

'There's a river ahead. If we can ford it a few times, it might throw them off long enough to put some distance between us.'

'To the river, then. And step on it.'

'Step on what?'

'It's a saying, you know … step on the accelerator … never mind. Just do whatever makes the horse go.'

'The horse is "going" already,' she said, sternly. 'And take your hands off me. This isn't Altima. You can't go around just … touching girls like that.'

'It's not that easy in Altima either,' Chamus mumbled, carefully taking his hands from her waist and hanging on to the back of the saddle instead. It felt a lot more precarious, but was probably less hazardous.

They did not speak for a while, catching their breaths after the madness of the chase.

'How much do you know about Altima anyway?' Chamus said at last, drawing a sigh from Riadni as she rolled her eyes. 'Fringelanders … I mean, Bartokhrians and that … always seem to be criticising us, but enough of you come looking for work in our cities every year. You talk about us as if we're all evil and immoral, like we're demons, or something, but then most of you seem to want to be like us. We don't know what to think about you. I mean, take the Hadram Cassal. What do they actually want … what do any of you want?'

Riadni was silent for a while. There were so many things that they wanted. It wasn't as simple as getting the Altimans off land that didn't belong to them, or stopping their businesses from acting like gods, although these were the kind of things that tended to aggravate people. And there was some truth to what he said about her people wanting to live like Altimans, but not the way he thought of it. She wished she had Rumbler's speed and strength, but she didn't want to be a horse.

'I live on a farm,' she said. 'We have cattle and sheep. The only time I see Altimans is when they fly overhead. You're the first one I've met. Normally, you're thousands of feet in the air. When I was young, I loved seeing your aeroplanes. I still do, really. I think they're amazing. Your people are very clever and they're incredibly rich, and that's how they became so powerful. And because you have all this power, you affect everyone around you. Which would be fine ... if you were as wise as you are powerful. When I was a child, I thought that clever was the same as being wise. But it's not, is it?'

She struggled to say what she wanted to say, but there was so much to it and some of it she didn't even understand herself.

'You're smart enough to control something as complicated as an aeroplane,' she said, finally, 'but you don't know to wash your feet downstream from where you drink.'

Chamus didn't reply immediately, and when she checked the road behind them for the trappers, she could see he was thinking.

'And the only way you have to make your point is killing people?' he asked at last.

'Some of that is revenge,' she answered. 'Shanna says that crimes on her people must be paid back in kind. That used to make sense to me, but I don't know anymore. You take revenge on someone and they've got to take revenge right back. It could go on forever. But some of it is because you're just not listening and the Hadram Cassal think they can make you. And a lot of people believe they can too.'

'You were going to join them, weren't you?'

Turning that decision over in her head, Riadni was suddenly reminded of Benyan. She had hardly thought about him since this had all started. Much as she hated to admit it to herself, he had been part of the reason for wanting to join. That, and wanting to belong to something more important and more exciting than farming, or marrying into the right family. She wondered where he was now.

 # EIGHT

A panoramic view of Bartokhrin and the Victovian footlands could be seen from high on the slope of the ramp that took the truck up towards the city's plateau, but Benyan Akhna could not see it from the dark confines of the cargo compartment. He was muttering incessantly to himself and the expression on his face changed like the rippling of water. Daruth, the man who had sealed Benyan into the bottom of a box and now sat with him in the back of the container truck, watched the haunted sixteen-year-old uneasily out of the corner of his eye. Transporting these martyrs was always a risk, but especially so when they were this unaware. The ones who had lost the capacity to even act normally were the worst. Not so much human beings as ticking time bombs. These were often the most destructive when they reached their target, but the most difficult to get there. It called for great cunning on the part of the men chosen to escort them. They must someday find a way to bestow the Blessing in the cities themselves and do away with this risk. Despite the honour he achieved in his work, Daruth would be glad to be rid of this one. In the dim light of a torch, he stared at the boxes of tomatoes that filled most of the space between himself and the doors of the container.

'Checkpoint,' the driver called back through the small hole in the rear of the cab.

As he turned off the torch, Daruth felt himself break into a light sweat. He had to stop Benyan's muttering, or he might be heard by the policemen. Crouching down, he clasped the boy's hands in his and started to softly chant a prayer. It was one used by parents across Bartokhrin to lull children to sleep, and Daruth knew from experience that it also quietened spirits. It would give Benyan's own mind peace and he would stop struggling with the ghosts. The muttering died down and Daruth let his chanting go quiet, but kept the boy's hands pressed into his. Outside, he heard the driver being asked for his papers, but he knew that the papers were fine; the driver's cover was genuine. As long as they did not search the truck ... The engine switched off and the handbrake went on. He heard the driver's door open. They were coming around the back. Taking one hand from Benyan's he drew the grenade from his jacket pocket. He would take them all with him if he was found.

The doors opened and light filtered through over the tightly packed stacks of boxes. The suspension settled a fraction as someone stood on the tailgate to look in. Then the truck lifted ever so slightly again and the light disappeared as the doors closed.

Daruth breathed out slowly and replaced the grenade. The truck started off and as he let go of Benyan's hand, the muttered argument gained strength again. Daruth gazed down in the pitch-black darkness. He would be glad to be rid of this one.

+ + + +

Riadni brought Rumbler to a halt. Over the horse's panting, she could hear the sounds of hooves again. But they were not behind her; they were off to her left. She cast her mind back over the course the road had taken. Had it curved around to the left? There could be a short cut from the village that came out further up the road. If there were, the trappers would surely know about it. She hesitated, unsure of what to do next.

'We can't go back,' Chamus said softly, reading her thoughts. 'We could cut into the woods ...'

'That would slow us down,' she shook her head. 'They know this area, if we try to hide we'll lose our lead and they'll find our trail and catch us for sure. No, we've got to go for the river.'

Chamus didn't argue, satisfied that she was making the right decision. Shifting around on the saddle, he tried to ease the flat pain in his buttocks. He had never been saddle-sore before and he considered it a bit much, given everything else he was going through. He switched the machete from his right to his left hand, wishing he had a scabbard to carry it in.

Riadni set Rumbler off at a faster pace. They rode down into a dell, where lush grass, sheltered from the full heat of the sun by the tall trees, lay in a thick, green carpet. A rocky bluff stood off to their left and just as Chamus looked up at it, he heard a spinning whirr and Riadni reflexively raised one arm. The centre of the belasto struck him on the neck, nearly pulling him from the horse as the long cords twisted around him and caught Riadni too, slamming their heads against each other and binding their necks together at lightning speed. Only Riadni's raised hand, caught now against her neck, stopped the cords from strangling them. She goaded Rumbler into a gallop and it was all she could do to hold on with her back painfully arched and one hand trapped. Her breath was getting shorter quickly as the cord constricted her throat.

Chamus did not bother trying to use the machete; it would be too unwieldy. He slid it onto his lap and reached around Riadni's waist instead, pulling her knife from its scabbard and sliding it up behind the cord between the back of her head and his cheek. With the rocking motion of the horse he risked slashing his face, but in seconds he had the cords cut. He caught one of the cords, letting the rest of the belasto fall away and Riadni heaved in a breath of air as she got her other hand on the reins. Chamus got her knife back into its sheath and drew out the machete just moments before one of the trappers charged his horse down the grassy bank at the far end of the bluff. The hunter pulled a machete of his own, but Chamus swung the single steel weight of the belasto on its length of cord, keeping the man at bay with its greater reach. With no free hand to hold on, he felt himself losing his balance and tipping sideways. He heaved himself forward to correct himself.

The trapper saw him drop his guard and swung in, but Chamus managed to wrap the makeshift grappling line around the man's weapon. In a desperate lunge, he struck out with his machete with his right hand and scored a cut across the back of the trapper's hand. This time he did lose his balance and would have fallen back over Rumbler's flank if Riadni had not grabbed him by the front of his jacket and hauled him back on. The hunter cried out and let go of his own blade, his horse's speed dropping away behind them. Chamus lost his hold on the weighted cord as the man dropped his weapon, but was happy just to have managed to stay up on the horse.

He glanced back and his blood turned cold. There were four more men on horseback following them. He nudged Riadni and she stole a look behind them. They came to where the road crossed the river … and Rumbler came to a stuttering halt. They had run out of road. The river was crossed by a ferry and the long raft was on the other side. Two ropes ran the width of the river, obviously for pulling the ferry across, but they would never have enough time.

'Cut the ropes,' Riadni told him, looking downstream.

'What?'

'Cut the *ropes*. It's no good to us. Make sure *they* can't use it either.'

He swung the machete against the post that anchored the ropes, cutting first one, then the other. The ends of the ropes drifted out and down into the current. Riadni turned Rumbler to the right and they galloped down the bank, following the flow of the water. Ahead of them, the banks on either side rose and the river narrowed and became faster. Riadni angled away from the rise, putting some distance between them and the bank. Then she stopped and turned the horse towards the river. Behind them the drumming of hooves drew closer.

'That is too far,' Chamus shook his head, looking at the far bank. 'We won't make it.'

'I don't know what else to do,' she said, and heeled Rumbler's flanks. The horse sensed her urgency and threw himself into the run. They hurtled towards the rise, Chamus's eyes darted to the left to see their pursuers closing on them, led by the second trapper, but they were still not close enough. Rumbler launched himself out over the river, but just as he did there was a whipping sound and as his back legs pushed off the ground, he stumbled. All three plunged into the water and the fast current carried them away.

Chamus fought to get his head above the churning surface and saw the horsemen gallop up to the high bank and stop. Two of them fired off shots with old flintlock muskets, but succeeded in doing nothing but hitting water. Riadni surfaced, her make-up running down her face in long streaks. She immediately made a grab for Rumbler's reins, lifting her legs up in front of her to fend off rocks as she was carried downstream. Around them the banks became high and rocky and Chamus knew it would make it difficult for their hunters to follow.

They let the current carry them more than a mile downstream to quieter water and then Chamus helped Riadni guide Rumbler out on the opposite bank of the river at a clearing among some dark firs. The horse was having trouble standing and staggered twice as he waded into shallow water. When he lunged up and out, he was holding his left front foot up. Chamus winced, and Riadni cried out. The cannon bone was broken just below the knee. Bare bone protruded from an open wound. Rumbler flopped down on the grass by the riverside, exhausted, his breath coming in shudders. The remains of a belasto were still looped loosely around his hind legs, one of the cords and a weight missing. Riadni was cradling her horse's head and Chamus went to unwind the cord. That had been what made the horse stumble in mid-jump. He stopped as he realised it was Riadni's. He recognised the wooden weights that had caught him when she first attacked him. She had thrown it at the trapper and he had obviously kept it and used it. He glanced up at Riadni's heartbroken face; she had not noticed the belasto was hers. Unravelling the weapon, he threw it far out into the river.

They needed to leave quickly, but he didn't have the heart to rush her. He pulled the saddlebags and other bits and pieces from Rumbler's back and laid them out, ready to be picked up. He went over and kneeled down beside her. She cast a glare at him and he was taken aback by the hostility in her eyes. Caressing the horse's forehead, she kissed his muzzle.

'Bring me the saddlebags,' she rasped.

Not knowing what to say, Chamus did as she asked. Riadni reached deep into one and pulled out a pistol wrapped in an oilskin, along with a pouch and a sealed horn. Pulling off her wig, she wiped her eyes with her sleeve and then opened the horn. The powder inside was still dry, as was the pistol itself. Holding the weapon upright, she tipped in some powder, tamped it down with the ramrod and then dropped in a round lead bullet. She tamped that down, keeping the barrel pointed upwards. She handed the loaded pistol to Chamus, making sure he held it so that the load did not become loose, then she wrapped her arms around Rumbler's neck and wept into his wet coat.

When her sobs had died down, she took back the pistol, cocked it and held it level against the horse's forehead.

'I'm sorry,' she whispered, and pulled the trigger.

The gun went off so loudly that they both jumped. Riadni broke down into sobs again, but now Chamus was picking up their stuff. She said a short prayer over Rumbler's body, then stood up shakily and Chamus went to put a comforting arm around her, but she flinched and he drew back. She kissed her hand and pressed it against the horse's face, before wiping her eyes again and self-consciously washing her face in the water. She replaced her wig and then they hurried off into the trees.

+ + + +

They walked for some time, skirting the far edge of the copse of fir trees and following the rim of a vast quarry, whose granite walls bore the scars of explosives and heavy machinery. Riadni did not speak, and Chamus let her be, walking behind her so that she could grieve in peace. Instead, he used the time to take in the country around him, admiring the dramatic forests and steep, spilling slopes and noting the damage that had been done by mining and timber operations. The wild landscape was marred in every direction by swathes of cleared forest and deep quarries and open strips cut into the hills. He knew heavy rain would widen those scars and wash away precious soil and he wondered how much of this had been done by Altiman companies who had left without cleaning up their messes.

They walked a trail of dry mud that had been baked hard in the summer sun and left little or no sign that they had passed that way. Every now and then, Chamus turned to study the land behind them, but could see nobody. Riadni's decision to cut the ropes on the ferry had been smart, it must have slowed them down, having to find another place to cross, but they would have heard the pistol shot, and sooner or later they would find Rumbler's body and know that their prey was now on foot.

A few times during the day he saw aircraft – two airships, probably carrying tourists out to see the wilds of Bartokhrin from a safe height, and a flight of five fighters, making a patrol. None of them was close enough to try getting their attention. It was frustrating, seeing his countrymen so close and yet so out of reach. He shifted the saddlebags over to the other shoulder, wishing he had a proper backpack and wondering if they could pick one up somewhere. But he did not relish the idea of stopping at another village.

Riadni hoped to find a stream to camp by for the night, but when the sun had dipped towards the horizon and they still had not come across one, they settled for a sheltered spot well clear of the trail, surrounded by blackberry and gorse bushes. The blackberries were still a pinkish red and not suitable to eat, so they used most of what was left of Riadni's food, some pork and beef jerky, dried fruit and hard biscuit. It left them both thirsty, but they were careful not to use all of their water. A chill set in as the day faded, but Riadni would still not risk a fire. There was nowhere to hang the parachute, so she rigged a tiny tent with her poncho and they took turns, one sleeping and one sitting up, keeping watch through the night.

SEVEN

L akrem Elbeth walked around the biplane, his eyes absorbing details under the early morning sun, his mind deep in thought. The seven bodyguards stood back, watching him in silence. Some letters stencilled below the rim of the cockpit caught his eye and he leaned in closer. It read 'C. Aranson'. A slow smile crept across Elbeth's face. Truly, he thought, this is a gift from Shanna.

He issued instructions to the men around him, sending two off for tools and another to relay further instructions by radio to the other groups around the country. If Chamus Aranson were indeed the boy pilot that Riadni had found, then he would be a great prize. It was vital that he be found before he could reach the safety of Victovia, or one of its outposts. To possess that boy would be to control Thomex Aranson, and Thomex Aranson knew a great deal about the workings of the Altiman military. Elbeth closed his eyes to focus on this new development. Its potential was extraordinary; he must make the most of it. His eyes flicked open.

'Baraya?' he called to one of the remaining men.

'Yes, Master Elbeth?'

'The boy, Benyan Akhna, must be stopped. Inform Daruth.'

The bodyguard hesitated.

'But he has had the Blessing, Master Elbeth,' he ventured. 'He won't be held. The urge to find his targets will become too great.'

'Then he must be killed, Baraya.'

'At once, Master.'

Elbeth tilted his head to take one final look at the yellow biplane. It already had a fine layer of dust from the field upon its fuselage and wings. He would see every aeroplane reduced to this before the end of his life. Man should not play in the realm of the gods, to go where they might look into the eyes of Shanna herself. Shanna and her angels would see to it that those who did paid for their sins of arrogance. His bodyguards moved quickly to mount their horses as he climbed up into the saddle of his palomino mare. He grimaced, leaning on the pommel as he waited for the pain in his hips to ease. His arthritis was flaring up and it made riding uncomfortable. Elbeth checked around him, but his men were looking away, pretending not to notice his weakness.

'Let's go,' he called. 'I want to visit Mocranen before I return to the caves. I think he will help us find his daughter and her friend, with a little persuasion.'

The riders wheeled and set off in the direction of Riadni's home.

+ + + +

Chamus woke up and stretched, his back stiff from the ride of the day before. He could see the light of day between his feet, and smell the oiled leather of the poncho just above his face. Wriggling out of the little tent, he found Riadni kneeling with her hands covering her eyes. At first he thought she was crying, then he remembered that this was the position Shanneyans took when in prayer. He waited impatiently for her to finish. They needed to move on as soon as possible and prayers were not going to help against musket rounds or machetes.

Riadni heard him moving around, but did not open her eyes when she finished her prayer. She was embarrassed that he had seen her without make-up the day before and had taken care to apply it properly that morning. But she really wanted to be alone, or at least to be with someone who would understand what she had lost. This boy from another world was too alien for her; the money he promised meant nothing now that Rumbler was dead. She was alone, with nowhere to go and no friends to turn to. But there seemed to be no other choice. They were both running from the Hadram Cassal and he could help her if they escaped. So she opened her eyes and found Chamus waiting there with an open map on the ground before him.

'Morning, how are you feeling?' he asked, in his usual, over-familiar tone, and then, when she didn't answer, added, 'I reckon we should avoid any towns or villages from now on until we get to your cousins'. What do you think?'

Riadni glowered at him, the contempt in her eyes causing him to look away uncomfortably. It took her a while to swallow her distaste for his presence and work up the will to tolerate him once more. They had a breakfast of the remaining biscuit and some of the last of the water while they planned their route. Riadni knew only parts of the land in this area and it took her a while to satisfy herself that she could find her way to Naranthium without using the main road. Chamus offered little in the way of advice and she was surprised at how readily he accepted what she said. All of the boys she knew would have scoffed at the idea of letting a girl plan a route. Perhaps Altimans were as soft as she had heard, perhaps he still relied too much on his mother, but the boy who had wielded the machete the day before had shown no sign of being such a milk baby.

Chamus adjusted the straps on the saddlebags, so that he could drape them over his shoulders, one on the front and one on the back. When he was ready, they started walking again. The chase of the day before had led them off course, out towards the west and now Riadni chose paths that would lead them back until they were parallel with the main road to Naranthium. Where possible, they kept to trails that offered the cover of trees or other features. Riadni set a hard pace, and it was nearly noon when they finally made a proper stop, finding a small stream winding across the trail that allowed them to fill the canteens and douse themselves in the cold, refreshing water. Chamus was tired, he was not used to such gruelling exercise and he was not wearing suitable shoes for the kind of terrain they were crossing. He had tied his leather flying jacket about his waist and now he cast it off with the saddlebags to allow as much air as possible to his overheating body. Leaning back on his elbows, he let his head hang back, so that he could stare at the sky.

'I could have flown this distance in minutes,' he muttered.

'It's a shame you let your aeroplane run out of fuel, then,'

Riadni sighed sourly. 'You lot are great as long as you have your machines to do everything for you.'

'Your lot will be doing exactly the same,' Chamus retorted, 'when your civilisation catches up.'

Riadni snorted.

'Why do you think everyone wants to be like you? At least we aren't helpless as babies without our tools. You must be pretty desperate to be relying on a girl to save you when your plane stops working.'

That last part didn't come out as she intended and she saw Chamus smile.

'Yeah,' he grinned. 'Things have just gone from bad to worse lately.'

Riadni looked away to hide her own smile. Chamus gulped down some water and lay back on the thin, dry grass.

'Don't you ever wish you could get out of this?' he asked. 'I mean, what do you want to do with yourself? You obviously don't fit in, I could tell that from the first time I met you. Aren't Bartokhrian women supposed to be seen and not heard? I thought they had to just serve the men and have babies.'

'It's not like that!' Riadni snapped, then held her temper in check. 'Under Shanneyan law, women have to be humble because they are made in the image of Shanna herself. Women are held to a higher standard than men. The man is given control because it is his responsibility to protect and provide for the family, but it is the woman who raises and teaches the children. She must obey her husband. But because she runs the home, she also has the greatest influence on the lives of the children and the future of the family.'

'That sounds like you were taught to say it.'

'That doesn't mean it's not true.'

'But you're not allowed to have jobs. Most of you don't go to school. You're not even allowed to choose your own husband,' Chamus was determined to show her the error of her ways. 'You have arranged marriages and …'

'Of course our marriages are arranged!' she argued. 'For both men and women. Kin comes first, over everything. If I married badly, it would affect my whole family. We all live with each other and rely on each other. A marriage has to provide for children; it has to support parents in their old age. There are so many things that can go wrong, but men and women must marry young, while they're strong and attractive, even though they don't know enough about these things. You don't marry a man; you marry his family and for the sake of everyone you love, you have to marry well.'

Riadni made an effort to calm herself down. She was sounding like her mother and it bothered her that she was making sense to herself. Chamus was sitting up, taking it all in. He had a large extended family of uncles, aunts and cousins, but he hardly knew most of them. They lived all over Altima, and he did not have to rely on any of them. The strength of family bonds simply wasn't a matter of survival as it was in Bartokhrin. What she said was true. It just wasn't necessary in Altima, where social welfare took the place of support from the family.

'We'd better get moving,' Riadni said finally. 'We won't reach Naranthium today, not on foot, and I want time this evening to find a place to camp near water.'

'We could do with some food,' Chamus added. 'I'm starving.'

'We'll get some along the way,' she told him.

Their route took them along a ridge, following the contours of a range of hills that allowed them to look down on the land below. She pointed out the line of white adobe buildings on the horizon that marked Naranthium, a good half day's walk from the foot of the hills. As they walked, she showed Chamus how to identify mushrooms, which ones were edible, which ones were poisonous and which ones sent you mad. There were also fruits that could be picked, leaves for stewing and for soup and root vegetables that grew wild in the land around them. She also showed him how to find bird's nests, explaining which eggs were best for eating and ensuring that they left a couple of eggs in each nest so that the bird would lay more there and not abandon the nest. A few times, Chamus went to refer to his survival handbook, but ended up just putting it away. Riadni wasn't surviving; she was gathering supper. They walked on, and Chamus's stomach rumbled at the thought of the food. But as the light began to fade, his bowels also started to vie for his attention. He needed the privacy of some bushes ... and he needed it fast.

He held out for as long as he could, but eventually his insides decided their demands weren't being met and threatened revolt. In a sudden moment of urgency, he excused himself and disappeared off the path. Riadni stopped in surprise as he stumbled away into the undergrowth, but then shrugged and sat down to wait for nature to take its course. Chamus sighed quietly with relief, squatting in the shadow of a hawthorn bush. He finished his business, embarrassed at nearly being caught out. Then he glanced around him, his heart sinking. He had used his handkerchief and thrown it away yesterday.

'Use dock leaves,' Riadni called from out on the path, a smile in her voice, 'the big flat ones.'

'Right, right, I know,' he mumbled, grabbing a handful of the large leaves.

'Yes,' she sniffed, 'I'm sure you've read all about it.'

Before too long, they were off again, clearing the trees of the upper slopes and winding down the hill towards the flatlands. From behind them, there came the baying of hounds and the echoing shouts of men calling to each other. Riadni went pale.

'They're tracking us with dogs,' she said to Chamus. 'They must really want us badly.'

They picked up their pace and jogged down the incline. The trail levelled out and they came into view of a group of large brick buildings that stood out stark and bold against the surrounding landscape. Chamus was struck by their design, for the latticed windows, slate tiles and the brick arches over the windows and doors were Altiman without a doubt. The whole thing looked out of place, here in the midst of the wild country. The path led down past the gates in the high wall and around it were poles with cryptic markings down their lengths. He went to walk up to the gates, but Riadni held him back.

'Don't,' she said urgently. 'It's not safe, look at the signs.'

'I don't know what they say,' he told her.

'They're warnings and holding curses. There's a disease in there. I've heard of this place, this is Falkrik House. We're not going anywhere near it.'

'But it's the first sign of home I've seen in two days. What disease? Who says the place is infected?'

'Do you see any people?'

'So? It's just deserted.'

'Listen to me. I've heard about this place,' Riadni urged him away, talking as they walked past it. 'The company that owned the mines around here, they built it. They had scientists working here, they were doing things with the rock that was pulled up out of the mines. They'd been here for a couple of years when people started falling ill. My uncle lived near here. He worked in the mines and he said that the scientists discovered a disease in the rock. Nobody knew where it came from, or how it spread, but it was the people who worked here who caught it; most of the miners didn't. They called it Falkrik's Bane. It made blisters come up on your skin and your teeth bled and you threw up and ...'

She stopped abruptly.

'You got diarrhoea?' he completed her sentence.

'Yes,' she whispered. 'Some people even swelled up, like corpses, only they were still alive. At least, they were at first. The whole place was closed down, and the people taken away.'

She was staring at him, her face turning pale.

'It's okay,' he reassured her. 'I'm just sick from the water. We're warned about it when we travel. Ours is sterilised with chemicals, so we're not used to the water in other countries. It's not a monster disease; it's just the runs.'

Even as he said it, he wondered if the disease they had found in the rocks could be carried in the water. He shook his head. They had been drinking the water in the hills above Falkrik. Water didn't flow uphill. He stopped and examined the buildings, remembering the reports of a plague in Bartokhrin and the conversation he had heard from the railway room came back to him. The two strangers had talked to his grandfather about a disease like the one Riadni described. And they had said it was already spreading.

'You know, now that you mention it,' he said, 'I've heard about something like this recently. Maybe we should get out of here. Better safe than sorry, yeah?'

 Six

Daruth looked at the message scrawled on the piece of paper and held his breath. They had hidden out in a basement flat in an unremarkable terraced street, where he had put Benyan to rest in a room with no windows. After the hazardous journey, they were relatively safe there ... and now this. The message was quite clear. The Blessed boy was to be killed. He had never heard of such an instruction before. Why would they go to all this trouble, only to kill him now?

'Master Elbeth has said it must be done,' said Helthan, the man who had handed him the message, 'and that you are to contact Thomex Aranson yourself.'

Daruth looked up sharply.

'Not to execute him,' Helthan assured him, 'simply to deliver a message. We have the man's grandson. From now on, the old man will be our eyes and ears in the military. Your instructions are in the envelope.'

A smile spread across Daruth's face. It was a master stroke. To have a spy so high up in the ranks, what an opportunity! He turned his mind to Benyan's death. It would have to be sudden. If Benyan suspected that they were trying to stop him from completing his task, he could be dangerous. And the Blessed had uncanny senses. The thought of bearing the brunt of a martyr spirit's revenge sent a shiver down his spine.

'See to the boy ... make sure it's done before I get back,' he told Helthan and the other man with them. 'I want to get out of here as soon as I return. Be quick, don't give him a chance to anticipate you. I am off to see Mr Aranson.'

Benyan sat in his room, chanting in one voice and then another as the ghosts passed control between them. The man who had sung the lullaby prayer was outside, he could sense him with two others. He could not tell how this sense worked, but it was as if he could smell souls, through doors or even walls. Their position could be marked and followed without any effort at all. Even now, he knew one was leaving the building and the other two were coming towards him. His eyes snapped open.

The atmosphere had changed, the men who had been leading him to his target were about to stand in his way. He lurched up off the floor and threw himself against the wall next the door. The door burst open and the one named Helthan fired a pistol at the point where Benyan had been sitting. The pistol had a silencer that muffled the shot. The moment he saw that Benyan had moved, Helthan turned reflexively and got off one more shot right in Benyan's face. The bullet merely grazed his skull, but the muzzle flash scorched his face, blinding him. Benyan barely felt it. He was already reaching out and seizing Helthan's jaw, his limbs moving like a puppet's as the Lenttons manipulated him. A twist of his wrist snapped the man's neck and he threw him across the room. The other man ducked in through the doorway. There was the sound of three silenced shots and Benyan felt two impacts in his chest and one in his hip. But the Lenttons lashed out, a bone in his left wrist cracked as it bent the barrel of the gun, then he slammed his right fist into the man's sternum, breaking it. His hands grabbed the sides of the man's head and he charged forward until they hit the far wall, his attacker's skull taking the full force of the impact. When he slumped to the floor, Benyan felt the life leave the man's body.

Even as it did, Benyan himself collapsed. He had been badly damaged. The will of the ghosts urged him on to his target, but his body was failing. He could hear a bubbling in his chest and felt bone grinding against bone in his hip. He dragged himself blindly across the floor of the flat, but his strength finally gave out under the front window that faced a light-well below the street. He clung desperately to the image of the two men and the boy, the rage of the ghosts bruising his spirit, but it did not matter now. He had failed Shanna. He had lost paradise.

+ + + +

The voice on the telephone had a Bartokhrian accent and Thomex immediately sensed that it was the voice of a man with purpose, someone serious.

'Thomex Aranson?'

'Yes?'

'Listen carefully. Do not interrupt. We have your grand-son. He landed his little yellow biplane in a field when he ran out of fuel. He is now in our hands. He will suffer if you do not do as we say. He will suffer if you try to involve the authorities. He will suffer if you try to deceive us in any way. Say "yes" if you understand.'

'Yes.'

'Good. Be in the Victovian Commerce Museum in one hour. Be alone.'

There was a click and then the dull tone that told him the other end had disconnected. Thomex put the receiver back on its hook. He sat there for a few minutes, deliberating. Then he picked up the phone again. Two minutes later, he put on his hat and coat and wheeled himself out of the office. One of the company drivers helped him into a car and drove him to Stock Market Square, leaving him outside the Commerce Museum. He rolled himself in and stopped in the main aisle by the telegraph exhibit. It was nearly closing time and there were very few people there.

After he had finished pretending to read the narrative for that exhibit, he started pretending to read the one for the elevated railway. A man came up behind him, acting as if he was reading over Thomex's shoulder.

'Don't look around. Just listen. I am putting a piece of paper in your pocket. It has a radio wavelength, frequency and instructions for the use of a code. You will use these instructions to inform us of any military operations that will affect the Hadram Cassal. Any violence suffered by our people from now on will be visited upon your grandson. There will be further instructions in the future, but that is all for now. Say "yes" if you understand.'

'Yes.'

'Good. We'll be hearing from you, Mister Aranson.'

Thomex waited for a minute and then looked around. The man was gone.

+ + + +

They had not heard the dogs or any other sign of pursuit for some time. The night was clear and well lit by the moon, so they kept walking after dark, careful to avoid any farms or other settlements that they came across. When they came to a stream, they waded up and down it for several hundred yards, getting out and back in again to leave a few false trails before following it east as far as they could and then settling down for the night at a bend where the water grew deeper and trees overhung a small clearing. Chamus hung up the parachute again and then dashed off into the bushes as his bowels threatened once more. When he came back, he was surprised to find Riadni building a fire.

'We need to wash as often as we can,' she told him. 'Dogs find a clean quarry harder to follow. Wash your socks and your underwear too, dry them by the fire. If we're going to be doing a lot of walking you need to keep your feet and your … you need to keep clean and dry, or you'll get foot-rot and the … the other …'

'I get the idea,' Chamus held up his hands, 'although I think I'll wait until after we've eaten. Isn't the fire a bit of a risk?'

'We're sheltered here, so the fire won't be seen,' she replied as she took out some of the food they had gathered and prepared two pots that she had in the saddlebags, 'and there isn't much wind to carry the smell of smoke or food.

We need it, or we won't eat.'

Riadni took a burnt piece of wood from the edge of the fire and ground it down between two stones. She brushed the powdered charcoal into a canteen half full of water, put the cap on and shook it. Then she handed it to him.

'It'll help … with your diarrhoea, I mean.'

'Thanks,' he said and took it with an awkward smile.

The taste made him gag. It was like drinking burnt chalk.

The food took some time to prepare and Chamus was ravenous by the time it was ready. There was a stew made up of mushrooms, potatoes, onions, basil and some other herbs he didn't recognise, and to go with it they boiled some eggs and had some wild plums for afterwards. It was not what Chamus would have considered a lavish meal at home, but after a day of walking on an empty stomach, it was a banquet.

When they had eaten their fill, they rested for a while, then took discreet turns to bathe and do their laundry further downstream. With that done and the embarrassing ordeal of hanging the offending items out to dry achieved, Chamus took first watch. Riadni loaded the pistol and showed him how to use it, then spent some time in prayer before crawling into the tent.

The night grew overcast and dark and Chamus stoked the embers of the fire as a chill set in. His eyes were next to useless in the gloom, but he listened intently for any sound that was out of the ordinary. The quiet was unsettling and at the edge of his hearing he could hear the damned whispering again. It was barely audible, a breathy, haunting collection of voices. On the positive side, his bowels were returning to normal. Riadni's remedy seemed to have done the trick.

Careful to avoid staring into the fire and losing his night vision, he thought glumly about what his parents must be going through. He wanted to be able to tell them he was alright. He knew his mother in particular would be going out of her mind with worry. He checked his watch. It would be time to wake Riadni in another hour. He wondered what she would have been like if she had grown up in Victovia – probably just as stubborn and wilful, but maybe more relaxed; she always seemed to have a point to prove. He thought she would have made a good pilot. It was a pity she would never get to know the world outside Bartokhrin.

Chamus's head jerked up. He had fallen asleep. Something had changed about the night. Everything was that little bit more still, and the hairs on the back of his neck were standing on end. He slowly turned around, peering into the darkness, and his gaze came to rest on a pair of eyes reflecting the glow of the dying fire. Whatever the creature was, it was beyond the light cast by the flames. But those eyes were hungry and far enough apart to suggest a large head, which would have large jaws and be mounted on a huge body. The thing made no sound. But it was coming gradually closer. Chamus's breath came in strained, short gasps. Forcing himself to move, he reached carefully for the pistol, which stood with its barrel propped up against a rock. The creature prowled around him in a circle that grew ever smaller. It came slowly into view, drool hanging from jaws full of saw-like teeth, a high arched back bristling with stiff hair, a coat of mottled black and brown camouflage, ears that lay flat back against its skull as if to push its gaping mouth further forward. He wanted to call out to Riadni, but was afraid to do anything that might trigger an attack. He lifted the pistol, but had forgotten not to drop the barrel.

The small lead ball rolled down the length of the barrel and dropped out the end in a small shower of black powder. And with it went his life. He saw the dark shape of the animal squat, its powerful haunches drawn up and he knew it was about to leap at him. There was no time to reload the gun. Aiming the empty weapon, he cocked it and fired. There was enough powder still packed in the chamber to let off a small explosion. The beast let out a frightened snarl, turned and lunged back into the darkness.

Riadni's head poked out of the tent.

'What was that?'

'The biggest bloody dog I've ever seen,' he shuddered. 'I think we'd better get going, somebody's bound to have heard that.'

He held out the pistol in a shaking hand.

'And reload this bloody gun for me. Quick.'

They walked for another hour that night, lighting their way with a carefully shielded candle Riadni had brought with her. When they set up camp again, they were both tired and in bad moods. They went without a fire and the tent, Riadni bedding down under her poncho and leaving Chamus to take first watch again as penance for falling asleep last time. After his encounter with the howler, he was in no shape to sleep anyway.

FIVE

In the morning, they broke camp at first light and got moving again. They were only a few miles from Naranthium and Riadni used the time to explain some more of the local customs to Chamus, so that he would not embarrass her in front of her cousins, two young men who ran a farrier's, making and fitting horseshoes. She had no idea what Chamus did and didn't know and she didn't want to take any chances.

'There'll be a basin of water by the door. Take off your shoes and socks and wash your feet. Don't enter a building with your shoes on.'

'Right.'

'There'll be a prayer before we eat. Cover your eyes when you pray. Don't lift your head or uncover your eyes until you hear everyone say "Glahmeth", that's the end of the prayer.'

'Right.'

'Don't refuse food if it's offered. Thank them and eat all of it. It's rude to refuse food. Wash your hands before you eat, and don't use a knife at the table. It's a sign of hostility. Food will be cut up before it's served.'

'Right, no knives.'

'Eat your own food with your hands, but serve yourself from the communal dishes with the ladles and spoons. Never touch food that someone else has to eat. There won't be much talking during the meal, but afterwards there will be tea, and then we'll talk. Don't interrupt the host when he's talking. My cousins are not married, but if there is a woman there, don't speak to her unless a man introduces her. Never, never stare openly at a woman … you're doing it to me right now. You're not supposed to do that.'

'Right, sorry.'

'My cousins smoke tobacco, which is forbidden under Shanneyan law. Don't tell anybody about it and if they offer you a pipe, refuse it politely …'

They walked on, Chamus listening to his guide and soberly wondering if he would ever understand all the rules and customs. There seemed to be an infinite number of ways to offend someone in Bartokhrin.

They crested a low hill and Naranthium came into view once more. It was a medium-sized town with a population of several hundred and there were a number of three- and four-storey buildings in the centre of the town, which Riadni told him was unusual for a region that suffered from the occasional earthquake. All of the buildings were white-washed adobe with protruding rafters and small glass windows. Her cousins' workshop was on the near edge of town and as they approached, she could see riders outside in the yard. They drew closer, and Riadni stopped short, and then dragged Chamus down behind an overturned, rotting cart.

'That's my father,' she said, pointing out one of the men

on horseback. 'The man standing beside him is called Quelnas. He's from the Hadram Cassal. There are two of my brothers with him as well.'

Chamus groaned.

'So your *father* is in with these sods too? He's going to know everything you know, isn't he? He'll be able to guess where you'll go.'

Riadni was still reeling from the sight of her father helping their hunters, but she could guess what had happened. They would have promised to go easy on her in return for his help. They wanted Chamus. She didn't matter to them. Papa had no choice. Being so close to her family again made her feel desperately homesick and she yearned to just go home with them and go back to her life the way it was. But she knew she couldn't. Things had gone too far for it ever to be the same again. She leaned back against the bed of the cart and thought about what to do next. They had to avoid Naranthium. In fact, they had to avoid anywhere her father might be able to find her. She didn't know what to do.

'There's vehicles coming,' Chamus said. 'Trucks, I think.'

Riadni peered around the edge of the cart and saw some lorries leaving town in a cloud of dust and coming towards them on the road. Bartokhrians used trucks, but a group of them together was still an unusual sight in the countryside. Chamus squinted against the sun, holding his hand up to his forehead.

'They're flying some kind of flag,' he commented, 'a white cross inside a red one. I think I know it from somewhere …'

He frowned, staring hard at the approaching vehicles. Then his face lifted.

'They're from Advocate! It's an aid convoy. They're from Victovia!' he exclaimed excitedly. 'They'll get us out of here.'

Riadni looked back to where her father was, but the farrier's yard was obscured in the dust cloud. The aid convoy was coming up fast, but she had mixed feelings about asking the strangers on the trucks for help.

Chamus ran out and waved down the lead truck, which slowed and rumbled to a halt. A woman leaned out of the cab's window and looked down at the boy. She was dressed in a shirt and jacket, not in Bartokhrian clothes and Riadni was taken aback by the fact that she was not wearing a wig or make-up. At the same time, Chamus noticed that each truck had men hanging from the back and sides, Fringelanders armed with revolvers and semiautomatic rifles. He was suddenly struck with doubt. Were these Hadram Cassal who had taken over the trucks?

'Hi, you're Altiman, aren't you?' the woman greeted him. 'What are you doing out here?'

'I'm from Victovia,' he told her hesitantly, glancing up as another man opened the driver's door of the truck and leaned over to get a better look at the two fugitives. He was a tall, lean, hard-bitten man with long hair tied back and several days' growth of beard on his face, which was unusual for a Bartokhrian. They didn't go in for facial hair. Most of them did not even need to shave.

'Don't mind them,' the woman waved generally at the men around them. 'They're just guards for the convoy. They won't hurt you.'

'My plane ran out of fuel,' Chamus went on. 'I'm trying to get home.'

'He's the one the Hadram Cassal are looking for, Leynid,' the driver said. 'They've got people all over the area out hunting him and the girl. The word is out everywhere.'

'We'd better get you off the road, then. We're on our way to Yered, but you'll be better off there with us than wandering about here,' Leynid said to Chamus, her face going from amused to serious and back again. She opened her door. 'Hop in.'

'That's a bad idea,' the driver shook his head, 'if they're found with us, we'll be up to our necks in trouble.'

'What are we going to do, Paronig?' she asked him. 'Leave two children to fall into the hands of Lakrem Elbeth?'

'Better that than the whole team,' he grunted. 'I'm responsible for your people's safety. They'll put us all in danger. I say leave 'em here.'

'Oh, you are ruthless,' Leynid chided playfully, ignoring his icy stare. She then turned to Chamus and Riadni. 'Don't mind him. His heart was removed at birth and replaced with a hand grenade. But he does what he's paid to do. Hop in.'

She got out and stepped down, so that Chamus could climb in. Riadni followed more reluctantly. She was bothered by Paronig's hostility and did not know what to think of Leynid. She had never been in such a large, modern truck before either. The cab was big, but even so the four of them had to squeeze together on the leather seat, Chamus next to Paronig, then Riadni and then Leynid next to the door. Riadni was uncomfortable being so physically close to these strangers. It was not proper. She risked a covert glance at Leynid, fascinated by the way she was not ashamed to bare her skin and the fact that she seemed to be in charge of the men. It was alien and exciting at the same time.

'This is going to make things bad for us,' Paronig muttered, as he shifted the truck into gear and started it forward.

'Well, I'd hate to think your men were carrying all those guns for nothing,' Leynid said primly. 'We'll radio the Bartokhrian army base in Maskadrin when we reach Yered. They'll take them off our hands.'

'If we announce this over the radio, we'll have every Hadram Cassal group in the area jumping us long before the army can get to us,' Paronig shook his head. 'We're not going to say a word about this. Not a word.'

Chamus and Riadni listened to this exchange and looked at each other for a moment. It felt good to be among friendly people, but it sounded like they were still a long way from being safe.

+ + + +

Daruth sat on a steel-framed chair that was bolted to the floor of the small, bare concrete room. He had gone back to the flat after meeting Thomex Aranson and walked in to find Benyan dying on the floor of the front room. Helthan and Mance lay in dead and broken heaps in the back room, no doubt at Benyan's hand. He should have taken care of it himself. Armed men had burst into the flat a minute later and fired tranquilliser darts into him before he could turn his gun on them, or himself. He had woken up in this room.

He knew that this was not a police station and the men who held him were not police. He also knew that Thomex Aranson had betrayed them and the realisation surprised him, he would not have credited the old man with that kind of strength. His hands were handcuffed to a bracket on the back of the chair and his ankles shackled to the front legs. Daruth knew what was to come and he was frightened, but he focused his mind on nothingness, distancing his consciousness from his body. They would get nothing from him. A man in a dark grey suit opened the door and walked in, followed by another dressed in the same way. Both carried leather cases. They closed the heavy metal door behind them.

'I have two questions for you,' the first man said. 'Answer them and this will all be over very quickly. Where is Chamus Aranson, and what do you know about Operation Heavy Rain?'

Daruth was puzzled by the second question, but it didn't matter. He would not say a word from now until his death. The man waited for a reply and then shook his head with a resigned expression and opened his case, revealing an array of metal instruments and bottles of chemicals.

'This is going to take some time.'

+ + + +

Advocate was a charity which campaigned for fair treatment for the countries that did business with Altima. Leynid Lefburoc explained as they drove, that because Altima was so much wealthier than their neighbours, the countries they called the Fringelands were kept in a subservient role, without any hope of achieving true independence. In Bartokhrin, farmers and other small businesses could lose everything at the whim of Altiman companies. The Bartokhrian government even had to tolerate Altiman bombing raids on suspected terrorist camps, their own people, because they still relied so much on the good will of Altima.

There were people in Altima who were outraged by what was going on in the Fringelands and they financed groups like Advocate to try and counteract the damage caused by their own country. Chamus listened quietly. His mother was a member of Advocate and talked about this quite a lot. His father couldn't be a member because it would have cost him business with the military. His grandfather thought it was all nonsense, saying they were just after money and regularly argued about it with his mother.

Riadni did not say a word. To her it was like hearing someone congratulate themselves for offering a bandage to a person they had just slashed with a knife. The column carried food and medical supplies for the village of Yered – the village that had been attacked a few days before by the Altiman Air Force. She remembered seeing the planes dropping their bombs and how her concern then had stretched as far as having a good story to tell over supper. Now she was fearful of what they were going to see there and worried about the people she knew in the village. Despite her disdain for the well-meaning Altimans, she knew Yered would need all the help it could get; it was a poor village in an area where the farming was hard. A thought occurred to her. She nudged Chamus.

'Your aeroplane is only a few miles from Yered.'

Chamus sat up.

'Really? Then all I need is some fuel!' He looked over at Leynid, 'I'll buy some off you. You can bill my family. Then we won't be putting your convoy in danger.'

He paused, he had forgotten Riadni.

'What will you do? They'll still be after you, won't they? You could come back to Victovia for a while, if you wanted …'

Now that he knew he was almost safe, he was worried about her. His plane only had a single seat, but she could always follow later. He knew his family would be happy to help her in return for what she had done. And besides, he still had to pay her the money he had promised her.

'I don't know what I'm going to do,' she told him. 'I want to go home, but I can't.'

They fell silent for a while, watching the road as it rolled past them and under their wheels. Leynid and Paronig talked over the youngsters' heads about what they had to do when they reached Yered, which would be in the next few hours. Chamus shot a couple of glances in Riadni's direction, but she avoided his eyes. He felt bad that his problems were almost over, while hers were not, but was relieved to be so close to going home. And he would be flying again. The thought put a smile on his face.

He was not prepared for what he saw in Yered. The trucks descended a hill into the main street of the village. The first things that struck Chamus were the bloodstains. He had never actually seen large splashes of blood before, and the sight of the dried, brown-red marks on the walls and the ground brought him down to earth. There had obviously been attempts to cover it up in places, but the stains were still there on the adobe bricks, and where it had pooled on the ground, it soaked up through the blankets of dust that had been brushed over it.

He morbidly wondered what it would be like to have a wound so bad you saw your own blood sprayed on the wall, to feel yourself being so terrifyingly damaged. Flail bombs had been dropped, explosives that blasted out shreds of nylon. A flail bomb was not intended to destroy, although it could smash through the roof of a building before detonating. It was designed to punish and to mark the victims for life, so that they would be recognised wherever they went. It left hundreds of shallow wounds, and the injured would carry the scars all over their bodies for the rest of their lives. According to Leynid, nine people had been killed from being close to the blasts, but dozens had been injured.

The first person Riadni recognised was the doctor from Kemsemet, his clothes rumpled and stained, his face showing the strain of days and nights of gruelling surgery. Clearly exhausted, he waved them through to where they could park, and then greeted Leynid with a tired smile. One by one and then in small groups, other people came out of their homes to look at the trucks. Many appeared lost or dazed; others aimed hostile stares at the Altiman vehicles. Every building in the village had been hit and few of the inhabitants had escaped injury. There was hardly a single person without a bloody bandage or even untreated, open wounds.

'Stay in the truck,' Paronig told them. 'Stay low. We'll set up the tents and come to get you when it's safe.'

Leynid was already talking to the doctor and the chieftain of the village. They were discussing what needed to be done first. Riadni strained her ears to listen. She knew people here and wanted to know what had happened to them. Turning to aim a hurtful comment at Chamus, she saw him staring out the window in shock at the ravaged street. Leynid was unwrapping one child's dirty bandage to examine the criss-crossing wounds on his face. Other medical workers were mingling among the rest of the injured to assess the worst cases. Paronig was directing his men to form a perimeter around the trucks as aid workers started to unload sacks and boxes.

'I know what this is like,' Chamus said in a hoarse voice. 'I know what this is like.'

And he told her, in broken snatches, about the day his class had died. Riadni listened without a word. She knew he was ashamed of what he saw through the window, that he was trying to explain why the aeroplanes had come here, but that he also needed to tell her about his own loss. Mostly though, he was talking because the situation was so big and so brutal that there was no way to make sense of it and she felt it too. She put a tentative hand on his shoulder as he finished his story.

'This is just going to keep going, isn't it?' he looked around at her. 'Look at them all. There's lads out there my age, and all they're going to be thinking is who to make pay for all this. I know what this is like.'

# FOUR

Darkness fell, and Paronig eventually came to lead them to one of the large tents where supper was being prepared for the aid workers. They were careful not to let the two youngsters be seen. They joined in the meal, which was eaten in Bartokhrian style, with lots of meat and rice and spices. The tone was quite lively considering how they had spent the last few hours and Paronig and his men even shared the occasional dirty joke. Chamus was shocked at first, but then realised that this was only the second time he had seen such a situation. These people lived with it everyday.

'Tomorrow,' Leynid told them, 'Paronig will take you to your plane. He'll make sure it's safe and help you fuel it up. Riadni, you can stay with us for a while if you want. As you can see, we have a few Bartokhrian women in our group, and in normal dress and better make-up we can keep you hidden. We could do with another pair of hands to help out.'

Riadni smiled shyly and thanked her. The prospect of spending time with Leynid and being among these people was the best thing she had heard in some time. Chamus was relieved too. A glance at Paronig confirmed that the sooner this young Altiman was gone, the better. Chamus wondered how he was going to be able to pay Riadni, but they would figure something out.

Leynid tore up some bread and smeared it in a garlic and tomato sauce on her plate. Chamus watched how everyone ate, using their fingers, with no cutlery, which was practical for this kind of food, but messy. The meat and wide array of marinated vegetables were easy to handle, but the rice was tricky. There was no butter or cheese, Leynid told him that Bartokhrians did not eat them because they could not digest anything made from milk or cream. There were a lot of strong spices, such as ginger, coriander and chilli, which were used as flavouring and preservatives, especially in the summer. The smells were rich and varied.

'We've been hearing of an outbreak around Yered and Kemsemet,' Leynid said to Riadni. 'Do you know exactly where it is?'

'What do you mean? Like a disease?'

'Yes, some highly contagious bug that's going around.'

'I haven't heard anything about it,' Riadni frowned, 'and it's the kind of news that would get around quick enough. Where have you heard about it?'

'Just rumours, really. A doctor in Victovia told me about it. I said I'd check it out,' Leynid shrugged, biting into a pork rib. 'The doctor here didn't know anything about it either.'

'I heard rumours like that,' Chamus put in, 'about a disease that causes bleeding and vomiting and all sorts of other stuff ...' he looked at Riadni, 'kind of like the one we were talking about before.'

'Falkrik's Bane,' she mumbled, chewing on a mouthful of rice.

'Right.'

'The Falkrik House thing?' Leynid paused, the rib halfway to her mouth. 'That wasn't a disease, that was radiation sickness.'

'What's that?' Chamus asked.

'Most elements release these kinds of invisible rays,' Leynid explained, 'but they tend to be pretty weak. You can't see them or feel them and they have no effect on anything. But some materials, when they're in their pure state, give off so much of this stuff that it can damage your body's cells. In strong doses it can even kill you. And you wouldn't even know it was happening until it was too late. They were working with one of those elements at Falkrik. They called it radium, got it from the mines nearby in this black crystalline stuff called pitchblende. They were refining it, trying to come up with ways of using these rays. You see they pass through almost anything – metal, stone, you name it. Problem was, the geologists didn't know the dangers. They were some of the first to experiment with radiation, and they died before anyone even knew that it could kill. They were using radium, but there are other kinds too, even stronger ones. One scientist thinks he's found a way to take photos of a person's skeleton … while it's still *inside* them.'

There was silence at the table, even people at the other tables had stopped to listen. There were openly sceptical expressions on some of the faces.

'Well,' she said, offhandedly, 'that's what I've read anyway.'

Chamus was ready to dismiss the whole idea as the kind

of story he read in science fiction novels, like shooting people up to the moon, or monsters flying down from other planets. But he could not help thinking of the conversation he had overheard while in the railway room.

'Could this radiation stuff be used as a weapon?' he asked. 'I think the Hadram Cassal could be connected with it somehow.'

'Not really,' she snorted. 'You could leave it where it would just sit unprotected and poison everything and everyone around it, but who'd do that? It would be as dangerous to the person carrying it as it would be for their target. You'd have to be mad.'

There was another long silence. Chamus was gazing into empty space. Everyone else exchanged troubled looks.

'My God,' Leynid whispered, 'if the Hadram Cassal ever got hold of it ...'

'Would it make the people around them sick?' Riadni burst out. 'I mean, if they were near a village, or a farm, or something?'

Paronig looked up sharply, his eyes narrowing, and then he leaned towards her.

'Are they camped near here?'

She clammed up, sure she had already said too much.

'Miss Mocranen,' he pressed, 'are they camped near your family's farm?'

She did not say another word, but Paronig did not take his eyes off her for the rest of the meal. He was one of the first to leave the tent. Riadni and Chamus watched him hurry away. Riadni had the uneasy feeling that she had just dug herself even deeper into trouble.

After supper, everyone retired to where they were to sleep, Chamus bunking down with the off-duty guards in the back of one of the trucks, Riadni in the Bartokhrian women's tent. Chamus felt a little nervous with these men; they were rough and mean and had little time to be babysitting a lost boy. But they were willing to talk and he found out more about them as they chatted and joked and gambled on knucklebones late into the night. They were Altiman-trained, Bartokhrian soldiers, loaned to Advocate to guard the column of trucks, and they were proud of their role. Each man was an experienced fighter and they would all be needed if a group such as the Hadram Cassal, or any one of the dozen other rebel gangs, tried to take the valuable supplies by force. They did not wear uniforms, dressing instead in the same practical clothes as the terrorists themselves. Every one of them was armed to the teeth with revolvers, automatic pistols, semiautomatic rifles, machine guns, bandoliers and belts full of ammunition, knives, swords and any number of other weapons.

Tough as they were, they all paid careful respect to Paronig, who sat apart from the main bunch and leaned back against the wall of the truck with his eyes closed. Chamus had noticed that he only mixed with the other men part of the time. He had spent most of the afternoon at Leynid's side. Despite the way she mocked him and Paronig's cold stares in return, Chamus suspected there was a closeness between them that they did not let show.

He drew himself up nearer the security chief.

'Paronig?'

'Yes?'

'Have you ever fought the Hadram Cassal?'

'Yes.'

Chamus waited for the war story he was sure must come, but Paronig continued to sit back with his eyes shut. Chamus tried again.

'Do you know much about them?'

'Some.'

'Do you know much about the Haunted?'

Paronig opened his eyes.

'In the Hadram Cassal they are called the Blessed.'

'One of them nearly killed me once,' Chamus thought this might get his attention, 'in Victovia.'

'If he had been trying to kill you,' Paronig said, 'you would be dead.'

He looked as if he was going to sit back and close his eyes again, but then he went on.

'People who die violently are often held to the Earth until they find peace. You may have heard this, whether you believed it or not. In Bartokhrin, we believe it. These spirits are tormented by the violence of their deaths, and they crave the chance to impose that torment on others, even though this is not how they will achieve their peace. Their hate and anger holds them to the Earth, but it also gives them power. Some people have a natural sensitivity to them; they can pick up a feeling or a voice, or another person's dreams and they are vulnerable to these ghosts. They can be used by them.

'But the Hadram Cassal have perfected a ceremony that vastly increases this sensitivity. It draws these ghosts out of the air and implants them in the person. After the ceremony, the Blessed must be kept alone in darkness for several hours to cement the bond. The person is bestowed with supernatural powers and senses, but in return he becomes a vessel for the hate and vengeance of these spirits. It is called the Blessing of the Martyrs. Once they take hold of him, he is already dead, because his powers are drawn from the trauma of their last moments on Earth and before long he will have to release it. He can carry that fatal moment with him for some time, but the ghosts always, always demand their revenge and they do not recognise friends or enemies. They just want others to relive their deaths.'

'I don't understand,' Chamus said. 'How do they control them then? Why aren't they going around killing the first people they see?'

'The Cassal discovered a way to imprint targets in the minds of the Blessed. They would be given a personal item, something that belonged to the target. It could be a piece of clothing or jewellery. Drawings or photographs of the target are the best, taken by someone who loves them; it leaves a powerful imprint. The target stays in the mind of the Blessed and often it is the only thing he has left after the ghosts take over. His will sets the ghosts on the target, and they release their death upon that person and everyone around them.'

Chamus went cold. The photograph that went missing from his locker ... He shook his head. It was too far-fetched, the whole thing – the ghosts, the mystic ceremony – it was rubbish. But he had seen it. He had lived through it. No, he decided, you could read too much into these things. There was a simpler, more scientific explanation. There had to be.

'Sounds like a load of superstition to me,' he said. 'How do you know so much about it?'

'My brother is a priest in the Hadram Cassal,' Paronig replied.

Chamus waited to be told he had been the butt of a joke. When the security chief calmly returned his stare, he turned away and crawled back to his spot at the front of the truck. Laying his head down, using his rolled-up jacket as a pillow, he pulled his blanket up around him and fell into a troubled sleep.

+ + + +

Paronig woke him before dawn and Chamus quickly packed up his stuff. They climbed down from the back of the truck and made their way to another one, where Leynid and Riadni were standing, waiting with three other men. Riadni would lead them to the aeroplane and then come back.

'Have a good flight,' Leynid said simply and gave him a hug.

Paronig started up the lorry and swung it around, stopping it long enough for the other two to climb into the cab and the soldiers to jump in the back. Then they waved to Leynid and drove away.

Riadni knew the area well and a mile out of the village, they turned off the main road and onto a track that led up through the fields. The main crop growing around them was tobacco for the Altima market, which was almost ready for harvest, but there were no workers in the fields that morning. It would be a few weeks yet before the crop was fully ripe. So the land was deserted as the sun rose and the rumbling engine of the lorry and the creak and crunch of its passage on the track were the only sounds to be heard in the open country.

In less than half an hour, the bright yellow biplane came into sight. Chamus leaned forward to look at it. He knew instantly that the field would be long enough to take off and his heart leapt. He was on his way home.

They came up to it from behind and he jumped down before the truck had even come to a halt. He ran up to it, slowing down as he studied the fuselage and wings for any damage, it looked alright … he stumbled to a halt, a puzzled frown on his face. Then he sprinted around to the front and held his hands to his head.

'Oh God, no,' he groaned.

'What's wrong?' Riadni jogged up to him. 'Isn't it okay?'

'Well, look. What do you think?'

She gazed at the machine for a moment. There was definitely something missing, but then she had only seen the aeroplane a couple of times. Then she noticed.

'Oh,' she said simply. 'Was that important?'

'It doesn't fly without it,' Chamus said through gritted teeth.

The propeller was missing. Somebody had immobilised the plane by simply unbolting the propeller and taking it with them. Chamus trudged over to the cockpit. The radio was missing as well, not that it would have been any use. He slumped onto the wing and lay back, one hand covering his eyes.

'Bloody hell!' he bellowed.

Paronig was out of the cab, sub-machine gun in hand, scanning the countryside around them with suspicion.

'We have to get out of here,' he called to them. 'Get back in the truck.'

Chamus was reluctant to leave his beloved biplane again, but they had to go. If the Hadram Cassal suspected that he would come back, they might have left someone to watch over the aeroplane. They climbed back into the cab and Paronig gunned the engine, throwing up dust in their wake as they sped away down the track.

They were driving down a section of trail where banks of earth rose up on either side when they came upon a boulder lying in the centre of the track. There was no way past for the truck. Paronig threw the vehicle into reverse, grabbing his gun with his free hand.

'Get down!' he barked at Chamus and Riadni, then to his men in the back, 'Lads! We've got company!'

Another boulder tumbled down the bank and rolled into the track, blocking their path behind. The truck slammed into it and ground to a halt. Paronig trained his sights on one section of bank after another, trying to catch a glimpse of their attackers. He could see the tops of at least four heads, but he had no clean shot. A voice called down to them.

'Give us Riadni and the boy and you can go!'

Riadni raised her head.

'Papa?'

'Come out to us Riadni, and bring the Altiman with you.'

Paronig looked at them, Riadni with her loyalties divided, Chamus frightened and staring back at him to see what he would do. The soldier gazed back, his mind chewing over his options.

'Get out,' Paronig growled, 'both of you.'

'What?' Chamus quailed. 'What do you mean?'

'I mean, get out. You're not worth the risk to me and my men. We have a job to do and you're not it. Now get out.'

He shoved Chamus toward the passenger-side door. Chamus could not believe what was happening. Riadni took one look at Paronig's face, grabbed the bags and opened the door. She stepped out and pulled Chamus out with her.

'Do you know what they're going to do?' Chamus roared at the soldier. 'What the hell's wrong with you?'

Paronig pointed the gun at him.

'Go,' he grunted and slammed the door shut.

Chamus fell back against the bank. Riadni pulled on his sleeve.

'They're not the Hadram Cassal. It's my father and my brothers.'

'What's the bloody difference?' Chamus tore his arm away.

'The difference,' Riadni said coldly, 'is that they don't *kill* people. They might still help you. You won't get any more pity from that swine, anyway.'

Chamus cast one more despairing look at Paronig and then miserably turned to climb up the earth slope to the top, where he was grabbed and his hands tied by Kinasa and Bowrin, Riadni's two eldest brothers. There were six of them altogether, her father and her three older brothers, as well as two of their cousins. Sostas strode up to Riadni and gave her a tight hug.

'You scared me like you wouldn't believe, girl,' he whispered. 'Let's get you home. Where's Rumbler?'

'He's dead,' Riadni said numbly, gazing at Chamus. 'I had to shoot him.'

 THREE

homex Aranson sat in his office, facing a radio set with the instructions from the Hadram Cassal in his hands. He read them and reread again and again, turning the matter over in his mind, looking at it from all angles. It was quiet in the office and he did not have the record player on as he usually did. The insidious whispering in his skull was intense in the silence. It was a Wednesday, but the offices around him were empty because of the holiday, Airday, when everyone took to the skies to celebrate the anniversary of the first powered flight. He was alone in the building, just him and the damned voices. His jaws were clenched together as he picked up the microphone and spun the dial to the frequency written on the piece of paper.

It was a hard decision he was making, but in truth, he had made it already. When he had set the G-men on the Fringe-lander, he had effectively sacrificed Chamus, but if the lad was in the hands of the Hadram Cassal, then he was as good as dead anyway. This way he might not be tormented. He was of no use to them, so they might as well kill him. Thomex told himself this, but it did not really matter.

Sacrifices had to be made in war. He had already made his decision. It only remained for him to let the bastards know where he stood. Checking the door behind him was closed, he turned up the volume on the radio.

'This is Thomex Aranson, speaking to the leaders of the Hadram Cassal,' he called as he keyed the mike. 'This is Thomex Aranson, speaking to the leaders of the Hadram Cassal.'

He waited.

'Aranson!' a voice crackled through the wooden-framed cloth of the speaker. 'Use the code! Anyone could be listening!'

'This is Thomex Aranson, calling any of the Hadram Cassal leadership who might be able to hear me,' Thomex repeated, 'and what I have to say will not require any encoding. I do not bargain with terrorists, not for anything. The man you sent to me and the others with him are dead. The same fate awaits any other assassins that you send to our country. I do not bargain with the likes of you, not while there is a breath left in me. My grandson is dead and gone. You will not make a puppet out of me.'

He turned the radio off and hung the microphone back on its brass hook on the side, heaving a deep breath into his lungs. Sensing someone behind him, he looked over his shoulder. His son was standing in the open doorway.

'What have you done?' Kellen asked in shock. 'Do you know something about Chamus? Do they have him?'

He stared into Thomex's eyes and saw the zealous fever in their depths. He strode over and grabbed his father by the collar.

'What have you done?' he shouted, lifting Thomex out of his wheelchair and shaking him bodily. 'What have you done now, you stupid, crazy old man?'

'Listen to me, Kellen,' Thomex growled. 'They were trying to use me, to betray our own. One of our people in Bartokhrin has just found the location of a key terrorist camp, close to where Chamus landed. Plans are in motion. Do you follow? Tonight, a glider will deliver an air strike over that area that will change everything.'

'An air strike? But what about Chamus? Have you even thought about how you might be putting him in danger?'

'This is no ordinary mission, Kellen. This comes from on high, from the men who hold the real power in this country – men with the will to do what needs to be done. In two days the Bartokhrians will be begging us to come to their aid, and when they do, we'll bring our army with us. We'll scour that country from top to bottom, and that is the only chance Chamus has. We can't bargain with these people. They do not respect anything but force. Only force can save Chamus now.'

Kellen snatched up the piece of paper that had fallen from Thomex's hand.

'They had my son and you weren't even going to tell me,' he snarled. 'This wasn't your decision to make. This isn't over.'

'Don't you interfere!' Thomex barked.

'Do you think I'd ever listen to you again, after this?' Kellen shouted back.

He pushed his father back into the wheelchair and strode out.

+ + + +

They had been travelling for about fifteen minutes, Chamus riding behind Kinasa, Riadni's eldest brother, Riadni behind her father, when they heard a droning sound. Riadni had been pleading with her father to let Chamus go, but Sostas would not be moved. The Hadram Cassal had given him a simple choice: help them find Riadni and the boy, or let his daughter pay the consequences for her betrayal. And though it shamed Sostas to do it, that was no choice at all. The drone of engines interrupted their argument.

Chamus twisted his head around, identifying the sound immediately. It was a pair of single-engined dive-bombers, Bellam Dragonflies, approaching from the south. Their hoarse, buzz-saw growl was unmistakable. His heart lifted, maybe he could get himself seen …

The two planes were flying fast, their up-tilted wings and sharp noses gleaming in the sun, the flyers looked as if they were going to pass wide of them to the west, but then they swung around and made straight for the small group. They swooped overhead and Chamus yelled up at them, lifting his bound hands in the air. They banked back around and came in again. Chamus was the first to spot their intentions. The smile faded from his face as he saw them position themselves for a strafing run.

'Get off the track!' he shouted. 'Get down, they're coming in for an attack!'

He threw himself off the horse and hit the ground hard, twisting his ankle, but he stayed on his feet, running for a ditch at the edge of the trail. The others were quick to follow, but Barra tried to pull his horse with him.

'Barra!' his father yelled. 'Forget her! Get down!'

The planes opened fire with their cannon, tearing four ragged lines of explosions along the track and the fields on either side. Some of the horses were killed outright and dust rose in a haze around the group as they huddled in terror while shells tore up the ground around them. Chamus cried out in frustration. Why were they firing? After all he had been through. His own air force was trying to kill him! The dive-bombers pulled up and away, their engines changing pitch as they climbed and banked in again. There was more cannon fire, and something white-hot struck Chamus's right thigh, and then he heard a whistling and tucked himself right in to the side of the ditch, his hands over his ears and his mouth open. Something struck the ground further down the track and a shriek like no other rent the air. Chamus was suddenly right back again at the airfield on the day his classmates had been killed. It was a sireniser, the noise blotted out every thought; he could feel the vibrations in his bones. Even at this distance and in the relative protection of the ditch, it was unbearable. He could not even hear his own scream. The mind-numbing noise seemed to go on forever.

It was a couple of hours before anyone could move. When the sound eventually died down, the Mocranen family clambered to their feet with ringing ears and trembling bodies to take stock of their situation. Riadni was near Chamus in the trench and she crawled up closer when she saw his trousers soaked in blood. He had been hit in the thigh by shrapnel and he was pale and in shock. She looked around for something to stem the blood, but could find nothing, so she pulled the wig from her head, rolled it up and pressed it hard against the wound.

There was a wail of misery and she lifted her head up to look out of the ditch. Her father was holding Barra's lifeless body in his arms, pressing his son's face to him. Kinasa was also injured, his left arm hung limp and bloody by his side and blood ran from his left ear. One of her cousins, Crivak, had been completely deafened. Riadni clenched her eyes shut against the tears. She could not handle it; this was all too much. She kept her hands pressed against Chamus's wound and started to pray for strength.

'Bring that wretch up here!' her father called out, his face twisted in grief and anger. 'Let him see what those bastards – the gods and their machines – let him see what they have done to my son!'

Bowrin and Poulie, the other cousin, jumped down into the ditch.

'He can't move,' she snapped. 'He's hurt!'

'Your brother is *dead*, by Shanna!' Sostas bellowed. 'Bring that swine up here, we are taking him to Elbeth!'

'He can't walk!'

'Then we'll drag the little bastard!'

Two of the horses had bolted, one was so badly injured it had to be shot, the rest were already dead. Using branches from nearby trees and horse blankets, they rigged stretchers for Chamus and for Barra's body and started walking. Chamus was conscious at first, watching in a daze as the sky passed slowly over him. Then he passed out.

✦ ✦ ✦ ✦

He woke in a cave. It was cool. An evening light shone in from somewhere around a corner in the rock. It took some time for him to remember what had happened. He lifted his head and looked around. Some men in Bartokhrian dress sat nearby, talking in low voices. They had not seen him wake. His leg had been treated and bandaged and was not as sore as he would have expected, but he felt weak and dizzy and slightly sick. His wrists and ankles were bound by rawhide straps to the stretcher on which he lay. He let his head sink back onto the ground. The whispering was back, crawling around at the back of his skull and it was stronger than ever. The voices were clearer and he was sure that some of them sounded familiar. He dismissed the thought. He had just survived another sireniser. Nothing he heard for the next couple of weeks would sound normal.

'So, you're awake,' a middle-aged Bartokhrian rose from the huddle of men and walked over to him. 'We were getting a little worried about you.'

Chamus cast a glance around for Riadni, but she was nowhere to be seen. None of the Mocranens was there. With a sinking heart, he realised where he was. Riadni's father had kept his promise.

'My name is Lakrem Elbeth,' the man told him. 'I am an elder in the Order of the Hadram Cassal. And you are Chamus, Thomex Aranson's grandson.'

Chamus's voices scraped the inside of his skull and he felt the hate and fear rise inside him. He pulled against the straps that bound him, but Elbeth held his hands to try and soothe him.

'You can relax, young Chamus. We're not going to hurt

you. On the contrary, we have treated your wound and soon we're going to take you back to your family. And you will take a gift back with you. Relax … sleep if you can. You leave at sunset.'

Chamus felt no comfort at his words. He suspected that whatever happened at sunset, it could only be something that the Hadram Cassal would enjoy even more than killing him. He turned his head away from the Fringelander and saw his propeller standing against the wall of the cave. It only served to make the whole nightmare more real.

+ + + +

Riadni was distraught. Her brother was dead, Kinasa badly hurt, Crivak deafened and Chamus would soon be dead too, if he wasn't already. And she felt as if it was all her fault. She had started it all. She sat alone in her room, still in the clothes she had worn for the last few days, wading in her misery. Somewhere in the house, her mother was sobbing over her dead brother. Kinasa and Bowrin had decided to join the Hadram Cassal. They would ride back to Sleeping Hill in the morning. Their father had not tried to dissuade them. He was down in the gathering room with Brother Fazekiel, who had come to offer what comfort he could to the family. She could hear them in the room below, speaking softly, the pain in her father's voice audible even through the floorboards.

Riadni covered her eyes and tried to pray, but the peace it normally brought her would not come. Eventually, she gave up. Shanna was not listening. She opened her clothes chest and took out another wig and a headscarf to secure it. She picked herself up and started down the stairs. Rumbler's saddlebags lay untouched outside the door, she took some things from them and put them in her knapsack. With a careful peek around outside, she walked out into the yard and off towards the hills. No one saw her leave.

Two

Chamus was lost among his whispers, the more he listened, the more he was sure he heard voices he recognised. He was sure some of them sounded like his dead classmates. He could feel their frustration and hatred welling up in him and he strained against his bonds. Then another voice came across, even clearer than the others. This one he definitely knew. He listened intently. It was different, it crackled and buzzed like a radio. It had static. Then it became clear, as if someone had tuned it in properly. It was his father. Chamus blinked, the voice was unmistakable, and it wasn't in his head; it was carrying down the cave from a radio where three men sat listening. He gaped in amazement.

'... I repeat. This is Kellen Aranson trying to contact the men who have my son. If you can hear me, please reply. Over.'

'We can hear you, Kellen Aranson,' Elbeth answered. 'What do you want? Over.'

'I want to speak to my son. Over.'

Elbeth motioned with his head and one of the other men

walked over to Chamus and dragged his stretcher over to the radio. Elbeth held out the mike.

'Dad?'

'Chamus, son, is that you?' his father was close to tears. In the background he could hear his mother break into a sob. 'Are you alright? Have they hurt you?'

'No,' Chamus said dizzily, 'but I got shot by a plane. I got its registration number.'

His mother cried out and he could hear his father comforting her.

'Now,' Elbeth took the mike back, 'his wound has been treated and we are keeping him safe, but his grandfather has not cooperated. I am glad to see you are more reasonable. You called us just in time. Unfortunately you have contacted us on an open channel without the use of a code, so you will be no use to us as an informant. I am sure that your security services are on their way to your house as we speak. Over.'

'Listen to me,' Kellen urged him. 'I'm only concerned for the safety of my son. There is a mission planned against you tonight, a glider mission. It will be completely silent; you won't hear them coming. I am telling you this so that you can save yourselves and take my son with you. Over.'

Chamus lifted his head. What was that about gliders?

'We are not afraid of your aeroplanes,' Elbeth smiled. 'What is one more bombing to a people who have suffered hundreds? Yes, we await your gliders, Mr Aranson. Let them come. Over.'

'This is serious,' Kellen insisted. 'You're in danger and my son with you. Over.'

Elbeth leaned over and looked out towards the entrance

of the cave. The light outside was starting to fade.

'Your son will be released to authorities in the Altiman flatlands tomorrow. Goodbye.'

He put down the microphone and turned off the radio.

'We don't have much time,' he said to his comrades. 'Tell the rest of the men to start packing up immediately. I want the camp cleared by the time we return from the Blessing. Tell them not to wait for us. Now, let us take our young warrior up to prepare him for his release.'

Chamus's mind was racing. A glider attack, it would be silent. No one would hear it and no one would see it in the dark – not until it hit. No, he thought, they wouldn't even realise it then. Not this kind of attack. The scale of the plan stunned him, it was not intended to kill the terrorists, at least not directly. He remembered the drawings on his grandfather's desk, the mounting for the glider, the compressed air cylinders. They were going to fly low over an area, spraying dust, radioactive dust. No one would even know about it. There would be no sign of it until people started getting sick. And then the Bartokhrians would not know what to do. They would have what looked like an epidemic on their hands and no way of dealing with it. They would ask for help from Altima and that help would be sent immediately, in the form of emergency medical services with the support of the military.

The army would roll right into Bartokhrin, at the request of the Bartokhrian government, and they would seize control of the area and then any other area to which they suspected the 'disease' might spread.

He reeled at the idea of it. His country was going to invade

Bartokhrin in the hunt for the Hadram Cassal, and they were going to kill scores, possibly hundreds of people to give them an excuse.

Two men came over and picked up his stretcher.

'You should listen to my father,' he called after Elbeth. 'You don't know what they're going to do. This is more than just a bombing run ...'

'You mean the radiation?' Elbeth asked, turning around to stare at him. 'The plan to contaminate my country, to leave hundreds of my people dead and dying? I know all about it Chamus. We have our spies in your military and it wasn't hard to put the pieces together. They will have found out that we are camped near Kemsemet and that will be good enough for your air force. They will seed the whole town with radioactive powder.'

He gestured to the two men carrying the stretcher and they walked out of the cave and started up the steep climb to the top. Chamus was taken aback. How could he just stand by and do nothing?

'But if you know about it, why don't you stop it?' he gasped. 'It won't work if people know about it beforehand. There'd be hell to pay if people knew about this. They wouldn't dare go ahead with it. You only have to get on the radio and start telling anyone who'll listen.'

'Yes,' Elbeth nodded solemnly, 'you're right, I could stop it right now.'

His face darkened as he climbed, setting in an expression of grim determination.

'But if you think there would be hell to pay if people heard about it beforehand, think about what will happen *after* it has happened … when we tell the world what Altima has done to us.'

The full impact of what he was saying hit Chamus like a physical blow.

'You're going to let it happen?'

'Of course. Think of it. Your country launches a new weapon on us, contaminating thousands of our people, its army sitting at its borders waiting to invade. When the truth emerges, there will be an uprising like the world has never seen. Altima will bring down the wrath of all the "Fringe-lands", as well as its own wealthy allies. And then there will be all the vengeful young men who will rush to join our cause. Instead of one or two Blessed Martyrs sneaking into your cities, there will be hundreds, swarming across your borders, bringing death to your doorsteps. Altima's great plan will be its own destruction. Praise Shanna for her infinite wisdom.'

Chamus felt sick. The stretcher swayed from side to side and he gazed up into the sky, watching the clouds scudding across from the deep orange of the east to the purples and yellows of the west. The whispering in his head was stronger than ever and his muscles knotted with hatred and rage. These men were insane, as mad as the men who had con-ceived the plan to release the radiation. Everything his parents had taught him about life, about right and wrong, none of it meant anything as long as men like these were able to steer countries with their insane logic.

They reached the top of the hill and the stretcher was laid down against a bank that faced Chamus straight into the setting sun.

'You are a privileged young man,' Elbeth said to him. 'You are to be the first heathen to be given the Blessing of the Martyrs. Normally, we would indulge in a more elaborate ceremony, but it takes a lifetime of religious devotion to prepare the soul for what you are about to undergo and we are somewhat pressed for time. Do you remember this?'

He held a photo up in front of Chamus's face. It was the picture that had been stolen from his locker, Chamus with his father and grandfather standing in front of the prototype of an aeroplane they had named after him. It had been one of the proudest moments of his life.

'You won't make an assassin out of me!' he spat. 'I won't kill for you!'

'You won't have to,' Elbeth said, soothingly. 'It will all be done for you.'

Chamus watched the five men make their preparations, his breaths short and shallow, his heart beating wildly with fear. They lit a fire and threw the contents of his bag into the flames, then tossed in the bag itself. His imagination ran riot, trying to anticipate what was about to happen. Images of pagan sacrifices flashed through his mind. Would it be painful? Would he still be alive afterwards, or would his body just be a walking corpse, steered by ghosts? Please God, give me strength, he thought. The men kneeled, covered their eyes and prayed. Chamus looked up at the sky again and cursed to himself. He wondered if they were doing this to torment him. But as long as they prayed, they left him alone.

He heard the word 'Glahmeth' and knew it was over. The men lifted their heads and Lakrem Elbeth kneeled stiffly by his side and rubbed something on his face. The priest then produced a stone mask from a bag at his hip. There were no holes for the nose or mouth and in the place of eyeholes, there were two purple crystals. The other four men grabbed Chamus's arms and legs. He was terrified. Why did they have to hold him when he was already tied? What were they going to do to him that would make him go wild enough to break his bonds? The strangeness of the mask filled him with dread and when Elbeth placed it over his face and clamped it to him by gripping the sides of his head with his fingers, Chamus screamed. He could barely breathe and he thrashed around, but they held him firm. Inside his head, the voices had suddenly gone quiet when the mask had been pressed against his face and this scared him even more. It was completely dark, then the shadow that was Elbeth moved aside and the sun's light shone through the crystal eyeholes. A purple glow bathed his mind and he felt a presence reach deep inside him. Then suddenly he was reliving the moment his classmates had died. He was standing at the door of the briefing room, the Fringelander was in front of the desk, Ellese was demanding to know who he was. Chamus wanted to warn him, to tell all of them to get out and then the Fringe-lander opened his mouth and Chamus saw the street in the town with the adobe buildings and the sireniser plunging like a spear into the ground, standing straight up like some kind of modern-day totem pole and then the sound …

The vision disappeared, the purple glow was back, drawing something out from him along the path of the light. He felt the voices then. They started from deep in his torso, rushing up frighteningly fast, filling him with panic and bursting out of him in a deafening shriek. For a moment, the sireniser was real again. Its detonation, carried back from some devastated village to be unleashed in the hangar's classroom, had been reincarnated once more as it was channelled up through Chamus and exploded out, the sound's shockwave crashing into the men around him.

The stone mask shattered over his face and he squeezed his eyes shut against it. Some part of him registered a terrible noise, but he did not hear it, as if it were there but had nothing to do with him. When he became fully aware again, he found the cords holding one of his hands was loose and he twisted free of it, wiping the stone dust from his face and opening his eyes. Three of the five men lay dead. There could be no mistaking the lifeless sprawl of their bodies. Elbeth and another were still alive, Elbeth sitting some distance away and staring at Chamus in shock and confusion, blood leaking from his ears. The other man staggered around with his hands to the sides of his head.

The man saw Chamus open his eyes and snarled. Pulling a knife from his belt, he walked over, the blade poised to deliver a backhand stroke across the boy's throat. There was a loud pistol shot and the man was knocked backwards. He toppled to the ground and groaned, clutching his shoulder. Riadni came up from behind Chamus, pistol still raised.

'Good shot!' was all Chamus could think of saying.

Riadni shrugged. She had been aiming for the man's chest. Still, he was down. She helped Chamus free himself from the stretcher and supported him as he stood up. He winced as he put weight on his injured leg. Casting one wary look at Elbeth, he considered getting Riadni to reload the pistol and finish the job. But he just wanted to get out of there. With one arm over her shoulders, he went with her down the narrow, winding path. It took some time to reach the bottom of the hill and he was pale, sweating and exhausted when they got there.

Standing near the mouth of the main cave was her father. He had a revolver in his hand.

'Papa ...' she started, but then there was the sound of a stone bouncing down the path behind her and Elbeth stumbled out of the shadows.

'Ah, Sostas,' he said, speaking very loudly. 'You've arrived just in time to see the true nature of your daughter. I didn't know you had it in you to raise such a traitor.'

'Let her go,' Sostas said, 'for the sake of our friendship, Lakrem.'

'Can't hear a word you're saying,' Elbeth held up his hands in helplessness. There was an automatic pistol in his right hand. 'You could say your words are falling on deaf ears. The Altimans sent a martyr of their own, it seems. Something had already planted the seed. Didn't see it coming. The ceremony brought the death out of him. And here he stands, untouched by it. I didn't see it coming.'

'Lakrem,' Sostas pleaded, 'there's no need for this ...'

Elbeth kept Chamus and Riadni between himself and his friend, but his eyes did not leave Sostas.

'I'm deaf, Sostas, but I can still hear the dead.'

Both men stopped moving. Chamus and Riadni looked from one to the other, directly in the firing line. Riadni turned to gaze into her father's eyes. Sliding her foot behind Chamus's and her hand up behind his neck to clutch his collar, she tensed.

Elbeth began to stride towards where the two were standing and Sostas started forward at the same moment. Sostas reached out for his daughter, but Elbeth was going to get to them first. Riadni threw herself backwards, pulling Chamus with her and the two men were suddenly facing each other, only feet apart. Elbeth, his gun hand coming up, was distracted by the movement for an instant and Sostas whipped his gun up and fired at near point-blank range. Elbeth's gun went off, but he was already falling backwards. He stepped back to catch himself, tried to aim his gun again and Sostas fired once more. The Hadram Cassal leader jerked as the bullet struck him and spun to hit the ground face down. He rolled over, but the gun fell from his limp hand and he gurgled a few slurred words before dying. Sostas calmly slid his revolver back into his belt and knelt to say a brief prayer over his friend. Then he turned and took Riadni into his arms.

'It's not over, Sostas listen,' Chamus said to them. 'I need to get to a radio, right now.'

'The Hadram Cassal are all gone,' Sostas said. 'They took everything with them.'

'There's a glider mission heading out here tonight,' Chamus told him. 'They are coming to spread a disease. You know the rumours? The plague? They are going to release it all over this area.'

'We've heard the rumours. They're not true,' Sostas shook his head. 'I haven't heard of a single case. It's an Altiman lie.'

'There haven't been any cases, not yet,' Chamus grimaced with pain as he stood up, 'but tomorrow there will be. The rumours were all being spread to set up the story. Elbeth knew it and he was going to let it happen.'

Sostas glanced down at the dead man. He scowled and then nodded to himself.

'And you think you can stop it?'

'The plan can't work if people know about it before the gliders take off. I need a radio.'

'There's none in Kemsemet since old Barark sold his,' Sostas said.

'What about the aid column,' Riadni put in. 'They have one. But we've no horses. They're hours away on foot.'

'Elbeth wasn't planning to walk out of here,' Chamus said. 'Where are their horses?'

'They weren't going to ride,' Sostas said. 'They were going to drive.'

He pointed to a small four-wheel-drive car sitting under camouflage netting near one of the caves.

'Can you drive?' Chamus asked.

'Well enough.'

They helped Chamus walk over to the vehicle, but before getting in he stopped. There were spare fuel cans on the back of the car and seeing them had reminded him of something. He limped into the cave and came out a few minutes later with a piece of polished, carved wood under his arm.

'What's that?' Riadni asked.

'My propeller.'

 # Oпe

i t took them twenty minutes to reach his plane, during which time Chamus told the other two everything he knew, or suspected, about the glider mission. The car's toolbox had the tools he needed to reattach the propeller and the job itself took very little time. There was no way to carry a passenger, short of lying one of them on the top of a wing, and he would not be able to land safely in the dark anyway, so flying to the aid station was out of the question. But if Riadni and Sostas failed to get to Yered in time, he hoped he might be able to somehow delay the gliders. Sostas shook his hand, then Riadni gave him a quick, timid hug, before he pulled on his helmet and climbed into the cockpit. He had shown Sostas how to spin the propeller, so once the engine was going, he waved and immediately started down the field. It was a bright moonlit night, but still far too dark to take off from an unlit strip under normal circumstances. It didn't matter. He had seen the terrain in daylight. It was more than long enough and there was no time to clear the path of any small obstacles.

He pushed the throttle forward, the engine bellowed and

the plane lunged forward. It bumped and bounced down the rough earth of the field, eventually speeding into a shuddering run and then he was up.

He peeled away and set a heading for the north-west. He had a map on his knees and he had already marked the most likely route the gliders would take. They would need to cut loose from their tow-planes far enough away from the area that the planes' engines would not be heard. He had flown with his father and grandfather in gliders and knew a bit about them. Flying a glider in the cooling air of the night was a tough job, without engines they relied on air currents for lift. The best route to take would be one that gave them plenty of thermals and updrafts on their way to and around their target. Like the range of hills that led down from the north-west to Kemsemet. And they would never make it back to their airfield, there was none close enough, but they would need enough lift after the strike to get a safe distance from the area. That narrowed down the routes they could take.

He flew to a point over an area of desert at the foot of the hills that Sostas had told him was uninhabited, calculating that if he could keep them there, they might lose their lift and either land or have to drop their heavy loads. Staying low, he hoped to catch sight of the gliders silhouetted against the moonlit sky. He flew large circles there, looking at his watch and waiting, hoping that he had chosen the right place, and knowing that he would not find out if Riadni and Sostas had succeeded until he landed in the morning, or until he spotted those gliders.

+ + + +

Sostas was driving as fast as he dared along the rough road. He could have cut across country on a horse, but the car could not jump ditches or fences, or scramble up and down banks.

'Listen to me,' he said to his daughter, 'when we reach Yered, I have to leave you and get back to the farm …'

'I'm coming with you.'

'No, you'll stay there. Send out the message. I'll come back for you later.'

'Leynid can send the message, Papa, I'm coming back home with you,' Riadni looked up into his face. 'I want to be with you and Mama and the boys. You can't stop me.'

Sostas nodded grimly, taking her hand and giving it a squeeze.

They jolted along, chasing the light of the headlamps, Sostas having to refresh his rusty driving skills as they went. They had been driving for less than fifteen minutes since they had left Chamus when Sostas suddenly slammed on the brakes and brought the car to a skidding halt. There, in the glare of the headlights, was a boulder blocking the road.

'Shanna forgive me,' he breathed, closing his eyes and laying his head on the steering wheel.

Riadni gazed in dismay. It was one of the boulders they had used to block in Paronig's truck. She had forgotten all about it. It seemed an age ago. Paronig and his men had moved the stone blocking their way back to Yered, but not the one behind them. Sostas would never be able to move the obstacle with only her to help. He threw the car into reverse and backed up the road. They would have to find another way.

+ + + +

Chamus had been airborne for nearly an hour. The night was still clear, but he was already doubting that the gliders would come, or that he would even see them if they did, for that matter. He could have been wrong about the whole thing, or he could have been wrong about the route they were going to take. The idea was so fantastic that he was not sure he even believed it anymore. And even if he did, Riadni and Sostas would surely get the message out in time. And the military were bound to be monitoring radio traffic. And they would stop it once they knew they had been found out. They had to.

He pulled his collar up. It was cold, and he had lost his scarf at some point during his journey through Bartokhrin. With all the waiting, he now had time to feel the weariness of the last few days creep over him, the hunger and thirst and the throbbing of his wound. The pain in his leg made using the rudder bar difficult and the exhaustion was affecting his concentration. But the fact that he was flying again made up for all of it. Something moving in the corner of his vision made him look around, but he could see nothing. Then he spotted them – three willowy, black shapes without lights, soaring above him to the north-east. He turned towards them, but his hand hesitated on the throttle. He had not really expected this. They were not supposed to be here. Even after all this time spent waiting for them, he was not sure what he was going to do. What if the fact that he was buzzing them was not enough to put them off? What if they were determined to carry out their mission no matter what he did?

He shoved the throttle forward. There was no time to think. He would have to make it up as he went along. He closed in on the three aircraft quickly. They spotted his bright yellow biplane with its navigation lights long before he could get to them and swung away to evade him. It was a waste of time. He had the advantage of power and speed. He swept in under them and climbed up right through their path, splitting their formation. They peeled away right and left. He clung onto the leader, harrying him by swinging to one side and the other in front of him and buffeting him in his prop-wash. Wherever the glider tried to turn, he swooped into his path to block him. He was aiming on getting it through to them that he knew their plan. If they radioed their base to report what was happening, they might get called back. Then it occurred to him that they might be under orders to maintain radio silence, or they might think he was just some prankster.

He let go of the leader and raced ahead to catch the others. They had not gone far. They were hard to spot though, their sleek black shapes could not be seen against the ground, he had to get level with or below them to be able to make them out. He banked left and right, trying to steer them round in circles. The manoeuvres were fun. He had never had a good enough reason to bully other flyers before. They were excellent pilots to stay aloft against all his antics, but he kept the upper hand. It was a little like herding sheep.

After a while, however, the gliders were still trying to make their way to Kemsemet and he was finding it hard to keep them together. He would stick with one and the others would split off and fly well apart from each other. In the darkness, they had the advantage of being able to see and hear him, while they were nearly invisible from some angles. He started to panic. They were not going to turn around; this was not working. He was going to have to get serious. The thought of forcing another pilot down terrified him, but they would be flying over inhabited areas soon, where he would not be able to risk bringing them down. If he was going to do it, it had to be now.

He banked hard, flying a circle round the nearest glider and came in behind it, slowing almost to stalling speed as he closed on the aircraft's tail. His propeller bit into the wood and fabric fin and tore it apart with a sound like a lawn-mower catching a paper bag. He pulled up before he drove right up the back of the glider, missing its canopy by inches. He could see the glider's pilot wrestling with the controls, spiralling slowly downwards towards the dark ground. Chamus thought his chances of making a landing were pretty good. He could not afford to worry about him. He sought out the next one and crept up on its tail. The pilot saw him coming in his mirror and banked away. Chamus turned with him, but could not slow down enough. He over-flew and had to come around again. In his haste, he came in too fast this time, so instead of trying to take out the aircraft's tail, he brought his landing gear down hard on the glider's canopy. The slim fuselage lurched and tipped to one side. Its right wing came over, swinging straight at him and smacked the side of the biplane. He pulled away in time to stop it dragging backwards and ripping off his tailplane.

The glider tumbled towards the ground, and he watched

anxiously as it disappeared into the darkness. He rolled over and followed it down. He saw it level out and swoop down into a field. He smiled as he admired the pilot's skill, but his smile disappeared when he flew over the end of the field. It was too short, and there was a deep gully at the end of it. The glider landed, bouncing a couple of times, rolling along the ground, and then, still moving at full tilt, it pitched into the gully and smashed against the opposite wall. Chamus swallowed what felt like a stone in his throat and gained some altitude. There was still one left. Weaving right and left down the bombing route, he searched desperately for the remaining glider. He switched his navigation lights off to make himself harder to see and flew lower, scanning the sky. There was no sign of the last flyer.

Chamus finally caught sight of the glider, catching thermals off a long ridge that ran in the direction of Kemsemet. He charged forward and cut across the black aircraft's path, causing it to swing over the ridge and down into the valley on the other side. He tried catching the other pilot's tail, as he had with the first glider, but this pilot was exceptionally good and was using his slower speed to jink out of Chamus's way, forcing him to fly past each time or risk stalling. Chamus surveyed the valley in the poor light. It was a long, narrow passage with steep walls of rock and thin soil. If he could keep the glider between the two ridges, he could eventually run it into the ground.

He concentrated on trying to hold himself on top of the glider, gradually pushing it lower, but each time he managed to force it down, he had to give up as his engine hiccuped and threatened to stall. He had to fly past and pick up his speed again. Each time that happened, it meant coming around again and catching up once more. He was losing ground. Each failure took them closer to the villages and farms at the edge of the desert. Then the glider pilot changed tactics.

As Chamus closed on the lighter aircraft, the air-force pilot pulled right up in front of him, nose up, slowing so abruptly that Chamus's vision was suddenly filled with the slender black shape. He found himself staring right into the other man's face. He jerked the stick to the left and rolled the biplane hard over, missing the other aircraft by inches. He stamped on the rudder bar and leaned back the other way to straighten out the roll, looking back, expecting to see the glider falling from the sky. But the other pilot had miraculously stayed airborne. He was amazed. Gliders were not made for aerobatics. He circled and tried to catch up again, but again the other pilot threw himself into Chamus's path, forcing him to fling the biplane over to the side to save himself from smashing straight into the glider and killing both himself and the other pilot. When it happened a third time, he pulled away and hung back cautiously. The glider pilot had raised the stakes. He had realised that Chamus would not sacrifice himself and had turned each potential clash into an act of suicide, so that Chamus could not tackle the glider without giving up his own life.

Chamus scowled, cursing to himself. One part of his mind had continued to think of this all as a game, even when he had seen the second glider crash. But now he was faced with failure. He had never considered any cause important enough to risk his life – that was to say, no cause that he was ever likely to actually be involved with. But now he tried to weigh up everything that would happen if this pilot succeeded and he found that it was so big, he could not even relate to it. Plagues and war were huge, historic things that seemed to bear little relation to this bizarre dogfight, up here in the dark. Alone in his cockpit, he knew it would be easy to turn around and let the glider go. He was a schoolboy who was supposed to be worried about homework and acne and embarrassing himself in front of girls. He had nothing to do with war and terrorists.

Then he thought of the people he had met in the last few days. Of Riadni, and Sostas and Leynid, and Paronig and the others and he thought about what was about to happen to them. Riadni's family was right in the centre of the glider's target, and she and her father would rush back to save them as soon as they had spread the message over the radio, how could they not hurry back to their family? In truth, he didn't even like the ones he'd met, and they obviously didn't like him. But the difference was that he knew Riadni, and he knew she and Sostas, and everyone close to them, were going to die if the glider pilot succeeded in dropping his payload. They would die slowly and painfully because two lots of fanatics could not sort out their differences. And so Chamus, who could not bring himself to give his life for the good of thousands, brought his bright yellow biplane high up over the tail of the black glider and banked hard, bringing the nose of the aeroplane to bear on the path of the other aircraft – to save the lives of a bunch of near-strangers.

He opened up the throttle, relishing the roar of the big, oily, smoky engine, watching the glider desperately jinking right and left to try and avoid him, but Chamus had learned from his opponent. He had learned the importance of committing himself to his goal. He did not try to clip the other flyer's tail, or attempt to herd him in a different direction. He brought his aeroplane screaming down at the cockpit of the glider, roaring at the top of his voice, the wind dragging at his face, pressing the goggles against his eyes. The glider grew larger and larger in his sights, and the pilot was looking up at him, trying to pitch himself sideways to avoid the oncoming biplane, but he was too slow and too late.

The biplane smashed right through the glider's cockpit, the lighter aircraft shattering apart, the crippled biplane plummeting on down, starting to roll, debris from the glider still being chewed and spat out by the broken shards of the propeller. Chamus's engine coughed and died, choking on fragments of its enemy, and the yellow biplane continued to tumble down into the dark silence.

ZERO

Vel Sillian was flying in a school trainer over western Bartokhrin, part of the massive search that had been launched for Chamus Aranson. On top of the official search and rescue teams, the Aransons had called on every pilot they knew, including those in Chamus's school, to join the hunt for Chamus's biplane.

Two days had passed since the now infamous gliders had set out on their mission. The first message had been heard broadcasting from a radio out here, an aid station in a town called Yered. That had been started by a Bartokhrian girl and her father, who had been the last people to see Chamus alive. The story of the gliders and the radioactive dust had spread far and wide, ham operators and then news stations taking up the message. The military had denied the story, and people believed them at first, but then the first glider had been found smashed up in a gully and aid workers had reached it before the military could. The lethal payload had still been sealed securely in its lead reservoir.

Another glider had been discovered, landed safely in a field a few miles away, with its payload also intact. There had been no sign of the pilot. Sillian was impatient. He had been assigned an area twenty miles from the nearest glider and saw little chance of finding Chamus. His schoolmate was now a hero, but two days after the event he was still missing and everyone was beginning to fear the worst. Sillian had been secretly impressed by the plan to seed the Bartokhrian towns with radioactivity, but now, flying over the area, he realised that if the glider had succeeded in releasing its payload, he would be in as much danger as anyone else should he be forced to land for any reason. Radiation did not distinguish between the good and the evil.

A spot of bright yellow out to his right caught his eye and he turned towards it. As he drew closer, he could make out the broken body of the biplane lying on the north-facing slope of a hill, the wings on one side sheared off, its cheerful paintwork covered in dust. He flew in lower, saw the cockpit was empty and swung around to see Chamus lying under the shade of one of the wings. Sillian dipped his wings, but there was no answering wave. He tried again, but the body did not move. Sillian thumped the side of his cockpit and was just climbing back up to look around for a place to land, when he saw the tailfin of a glider lying less than a mile from the wrecked biplane. He swooped in to be sure what it was, then opened the throttle and pulled into a steep climb, his heart racing. Had he got too close?

He checked the position of the biplane on the map and called it in, telling the search controller about the glider wreckage. Then he cast an uneasy eye on his fuel gauge, and not liking what he saw, set off for home.

+ + + +

Benyan Akhna's eyes opened, but nothing changed. He could not see. For a moment he panicked, but then the Lenttons spoke to him, reassuring him. They whispered into his mind, describing his surroundings. He was in a pale-green room, in a high bed with rails on the sides, a machine sat on a narrow wooden table beside him. The machine had buttons and lights on the front, and behind a rectangular piece of glass a line of light darted from left to right, zigzagging up and down as it passed the middle. There were wires stuck to his chest and a needle in his arm, to which a plastic tube was attached. The tube ran up to a bag of clear fluid that hung from a metal stand. There were curtains on the window, and it was dark outside. A small lamp was the only light in the room. There was a metal clipboard hanging from the end of the bed. His was one of a dozen beds in the room, most of which were empty; the rest held sleeping bodies. Benyan had heard of such places. He was in an Altiman hospital. So he was still alive.

Thomex Aranson was here, the Lenttons told him. They could sense him. He was here with his son and grandson. All three were on the next floor. There was still a chance for him to reach paradise. Benyan went to sit up and grunted. A pain lanced through his chest and hip and he fell back, lying still until the pain passed. The ghosts hissed angrily. They had listened while the Altiman doctors had stood over his body, speaking in hushed tones, astounded that he was still alive, if only just. They had heard the arguments that he should be allowed to die, that there was no hope. The spirits had wrestled with death, using all their remaining power to keep this body breathing, hanging tentatively to life in the hope that they might still wreak their revenge. They would not be stopped now.

Benyan cried out as a violent force sat him up and used his arms to prop himself as he swung his legs over the side of the bed. One hand went to his face, found a bandage over his eyes and pulled it up. He gasped as the dressing was peeled away from the blistered powder burn. But he was still blind. He started to sob, but the ghosts stood him up. He wheezed as another bolt of pain went through his chest and then he was wobbling on his feet. The broken edges of bone in his hip ground against each other as he started to walk, Benyan could only surrender to the will of the spirits. He sensed that they were weaker now, that their power was waning and that soon they would have nothing more to carry him, and he prayed to Shanna for that release.

+ + + +

Chamus opened his eyes. He was in a room with pale-green walls, lit only by a small lamp. He was lying in a hospital bed in what must be a private room. His mother sat slumped and asleep in a chair next to his bed and there were flowers in vases on every flat surface except the floor. He let his mother sleep for a few minutes while he gathered his thoughts.

He remembered hunting the gliders, but there were only flashes of the dogfights, and for a while he could not quite remember why he had been after them. His leg ached. He pushed the covers back and peeled off a dressing to see one large wound and a couple of smaller ones, all of which had been stitched. That had been the shrapnel from the cannon shells. The shin of his other leg itched and he pulled the covers aside to see his left leg in a cast up to his knee. There were scratches on his face and neck, his right forearm was bandaged up and he was bruised all over. A sharp pain in his side told him he had cracked a rib or two as well. Memories of crashing his biplane flickered in his mind and he groaned.

Nita's eyes opened drowsily and then she sat up. Her face lifted in a smile and she leaned forward and gave him a gentle hug.

'Hi Mum.'

'Oh Cham,' she said, her voice cracking, 'we were so worried. Thank God.'

He hugged her back, bursting with emotion and unable to speak.

'You're quite the hero,' she sat back, wiping tears from her face and trying to be more reserved than she was. She knew he got embarrassed when she got motherly. 'The whole country's talking about you. There have been reporters looking for you and Riadni …'

'You've met Riadni?' he asked.

'She's here,' Nita replied. 'She came with that aid worker, Leynid, when they brought you here. Everyone's here. Your father and grandfather are only down the hall, and Riadni and Leynid too.'

A nurse looked in the door.

'Ah! You're awake,' she observed. 'I'll fetch the doctor.'

She left and Nita turned back to her son.

'You stopped the gliders. The message went out all over the country on the radio, but not in time to force them from calling back the mission. The government is furious, all of the Board and most of the air-force and army commanders say they didn't know what was going on. But nobody believes anybody now. They're at each others' throats. But what matters is you stopped a catastrophe before it could happen. My little boy's a hero!'

'Aw, Mum ...'

He was spared further cringing by the arrival of his father and grandfather, who hugged him carefully, his ribs still objecting to overenthusiastic embraces, and more thanksgiving and singing of praises followed. Riadni came in then, dressed in a conservatively long, blue skirt and blouse that she had obviously bought in Victovia, along with an Altiman-styled wig and some lightly applied make-up. Chamus found it difficult to talk to her in normal surroundings with everyone else around, and once she had assured herself that he was alright, she seemed happy just to sit by and let his family do the talking.

He noticed his grandfather was very quiet too, and a little cold, despite his wide smile. Chamus wondered if anybody knew of the part he had played in the plan, but decided to say nothing. It would all come out eventually. For now, Chamus just wanted to enjoy being safe and back with his family ... and bask in the glory of being a hero.

'You had us absolutely terrified,' his father was saying, 'when you didn't turn up during the first couple of days, and then we found the first two gliders. We were almost ready to give you up for lost. Then, when your friend found the plane and spotted you lying there, but saw the wrecked glider at the same time, it was the worst moment of our lives ...'

Chamus saw his mother take his father's hand as Kellen

spoke and remembered Lakrem Elbeth holding the mask to his face, the feel of the old man's dry hands against his ears, the darkness as his eyes had been covered …

'Then Riadni here and Leynid led a group to your plane. There was a leak in the glider's container, but it was small and the wind blew most of the radiation away from you. The doctors said you picked up a bit, but they've been treating you for it …'

Chamus felt a chill as he heard the hissing whispers of voices, inside his head, but distant, and getting closer. Kellen paused, puzzled by the expression on his son's face.

'Cham? What's wrong?'

'There's somebody coming. Someone's coming to hurt us.'

He felt stupid and helpless, sitting there in the bed, crippled and afraid of something he couldn't describe. But his fear was catching. His mother leaned towards him. His father stood up and Riadni cocked her head. She thought she could hear a familiar voice from somewhere. Thomex, who was closest to the door, opened it wider and rolled his wheelchair forwards to look out into the corridor. What he saw caused him to panic, trying to turn the chair while still in the doorway. It jammed and he pulled frantically at the footrest that caught on the doorframe.

'Dad?' Kellen frowned. 'What's wrong?'

'Kellen, get back son! Get me in, close the door for God's sake!'

Kellen pushed his seat aside and leaned out over his father to look into the hallway. A Bartokhrian boy suddenly seized the old man's hair with one hand. He was chanting prayers and had burns on his face and bleeding wounds in his chest. He wrapped the other arm around Thomex's neck and butted Kellen in the face as the younger man tried to free his father.

Flames burst from the boy's mouth and hands and engulfed the old man and they both fell back into the corridor. Kellen was forced backwards by the heat, calling desperately for his father. Alarms went off and there were screams up and down the corridor. Chamus went to climb off the bed to help, but his mother stopped him. The fire blazed brightly for a few more moments, then seemed to tire out and die down. Riadni grabbed his blankets and she and Kellen threw them over the two burning figures.

They managed to smother the worst of the fire, but Thomex had been badly burned. He was not moving. The boy's arms were raw and blistered, and Riadni saw with horror that it was Benyan. She knelt down by his side. He was semi-conscious and mumbling incoherently. Kellen fell to his knees by his father and reached down to him, wanting to touch him, but afraid to. Nita came out to him and pulled him away, hugging him to her as he let out a trembling moan.

Medical staff ran up and ushered everyone away, lying Benyan flat and getting him onto a stretcher. Thomex was not moved. Two doctors solemnly checked his vital signs and looked at each other, shaking their heads. Chamus lay back and covered his face with his hands. The more senior of the two doctors stood up and turned to Kellen and asked them all to step into the room. He was a small man with a wizened face, greying hair and hard eyes. He closed the door behind them.

'I'm sorry, but there is nothing we can do for Thomex,' he

told them. 'I doubt anything I could say at this time would offer you any comfort.'

Kellen and Nita sat on Chamus's bed, holding each other. Nita grasped Chamus's hand. Riadni found herself left to stand in a corner, forgotten by the family and ignored by the doctor.

'What I will say is this,' the doctor said hesitantly, 'this boy was dying. He would not have been alive to do this if he had not been brought here and treated. Even now his life is hanging by a very thin thread.'

His eyes flicked towards Riadni, but then fixed on the Aransons once more.

'He could still *die*,' he said carefully, his voice intense. 'Despite our best efforts, the boy who killed Thomex could still die.'

They all stared at him. There could be no doubt about what he was saying. Kellen's gaze hardened and Nita looked shocked. Riadni glanced over at Chamus. She was stunned, seeing Benyan like that had taken the wind out of her, and now this. She said nothing. Despite hating the doctor for his offer, everything she had grown up to believe told her that this family had the right to make that decision. There was a long silence.

'I want him alive,' Chamus said, his throat tight with tension.

The doctor spared him a glance, and then looked back at his parents.

'Keep him alive,' Chamus insisted, the iron in his voice forcing the man to turn and face him, his gaze boring into the doctor's. 'This is why none of it ever stops. Because everybody thinks killing people is how you get things done.'

'This isn't our decision,' Nita told her son, before turning on the doctor. 'You do your job, Doctor. Save that boy's life. I want to ask him face to face why he killed my father-in-law.'

The doctor looked unsettled. After what he had seen in the corridor, he had already made a decision and now this family were turning their backs on what had just happened. The old man's son, though, he would want something done. Kellen was leaning his head on his wife's shoulder, staring at the wall. His eyes came into focus and he lifted his head, meeting the other man's gaze.

'I want him to know what he's done,' Kellen muttered. 'I want to change his mind, to make him see what he's done. He already wants to die. Why give him what he wants?'

The doctor turned and opened the door. He regarded them carefully one last time and then walked out, closing the door behind him.

+ + + +

Two months later, Riadni stood watching the red and white biplane coming in to land on the mucky road. It touched down, spattering mud on the undersides of its wings, and settled back on its tailwheel. Slowing down, it taxied to the clear area where the aid column had pitched its tents and drew up beside her. She waved frantically and Chamus waved back before cutting the power, sliding back the canopy and taking off his helmet.

'Can you stay long?' she asked, walking over as he climbed out.

'Just for a couple of days,' he replied, taking out a sack of letters. 'Dad's still nervous about me having his plane for any length of time. Says, given my record, I'm lucky he lets me fly at all. Here, I brought your post.'

'Thanks.'

He pulled a cane from the cockpit and leaned on it as he let go of the plane.

'How's the leg?' she nodded at the walking stick.

'Not bad, getting better.'

'You're just in time for lunch. Leynid's down at the village. She said she'd be up as soon as she's finished helping with the calving. Not that they need her help, but she thought it would be a bit of a laugh. Only a townie would consider sticking their arm up a cow's you-know-what a bit of a laugh. I think she's definitely a lost cause.'

'As long as she washes her hands before lunch.'

'How are your parents?'

'Holding up. The hearings have brought up a lot of Grandad's history. It's pretty gruesome stuff. Dad's taking it hard, but he'll be okay.'

They looked at each other, smiling.

'How's Benyan?' she inquired, hesitantly.

'Almost well enough to stand trial,' he replied, staring into the distance. 'Apparently he's terrified. Strange that … willing to die for his cause, but scared of sitting in a courtroom. He's going to spend a long time in prison. Maybe it'll give him time to think.'

He looked at Riadni, leaning on his cane and not saying anything, and she could see he needed this break.

'Ever been flying?' he asked her.

'You know I haven't.'

'Want to?'

'If you promise not to crash, maybe.'

'Well, doing it without crashing is the whole point.'

'You'd do well to remember that, then.'

Chamus helped her into the back seat and showed her how to belt up. Then he climbed into the seat in front of her and started up the engine. He slid the canopy closed, eased the throttle forward and stepped on the rudder pedal to swing the plane around.

'You won't do anything dangerous, right?' she said worriedly.

'Except for taking off, no,' he replied and pushed the throttle forward.

The engine's pitch rose and the plane trundled forward, picking up speed. Riadni clutched the edge of her seat so tightly her knuckles went white and her whole body tensed up. Then the plane lifted off and her stomach lurched. She closed her eyes at first, and then forced herself to open them. The land was falling away around them. She shut her eyes again. When she opened them again, the sky was all over one side and the land all over the other. Riadni gaped as the plane banked one way, then the other. Below them, she could see the camp that had become her home and off to the west, the farm where she had grown up and the land she and Chamus had fled across. From up here she could see it all together for the first time.

'How are you feeling?' he called back to her.

'Take me higher!' she cried.

He laughed and climbed towards the clouds.